# Love of Life and Other Stories

# Love of Life and Other Stories

Jack London

MINT EDITIONS

*Love of Life and Other Stories* was first published in 1907.

This edition published by Mint Editions 2021.

ISBN 9781513270104 | E-ISBN 9781513275109

Published by Mint Editions®

 MINT
EDITIONS

minteditionbooks.com

Publishing Director: Jennifer Newens
Design & Production: Rachel Lopez Metzger
Typesetting: Westchester Publishing Services

# Contents

# LOVE OF LIFE

*"This out of all will remain—*
*They have lived and have tossed:*
*So much of the game will be gain,*
*Though the gold of the dice has been lost."*

They limped painfully down the bank, and once the foremost of the two men staggered among the rough-strewn rocks. They were tired and weak, and their faces had the drawn expression of patience which comes of hardship long endured. They were heavily burdened with blanket packs which were strapped to their shoulders. Head-straps, passing across the forehead, helped support these packs. Each man carried a rifle. They walked in a stooped posture, the shoulders well forward, the head still farther forward, the eyes bent upon the ground.

"I wish we had just about two of them cartridges that's layin' in that cache of ours," said the second man.

His voice was utterly and drearily expressionless. He spoke without enthusiasm; and the first man, limping into the milky stream that foamed over the rocks, vouchsafed no reply.

The other man followed at his heels. They did not remove their foot-gear, though the water was icy cold—so cold that their ankles ached and their feet went numb. In places the water dashed against their knees, and both men staggered for footing.

The man who followed slipped on a smooth boulder, nearly fell, but recovered himself with a violent effort, at the same time uttering a sharp exclamation of pain. He seemed faint and dizzy and put out his free hand while he reeled, as though seeking support against the air. When he had steadied himself he stepped forward, but reeled again and nearly fell. Then he stood still and looked at the other man, who had never turned his head.

The man stood still for fully a minute, as though debating with himself. Then he called out:

"I say, Bill, I've sprained my ankle."

Bill staggered on through the milky water. He did not look around. The man watched him go, and though his face was expressionless as ever, his eyes were like the eyes of a wounded deer.

The other man limped up the farther bank and continued straight on without looking back. The man in the stream watched him. His lips trembled a little, so that the rough thatch of brown hair which covered them was visibly agitated. His tongue even strayed out to moisten them.

"Bill!" he cried out.

It was the pleading cry of a strong man in distress, but Bill's head did not turn. The man watched him go, limping grotesquely and lurching forward with stammering gait up the slow slope toward the soft sky-line of the low-lying hill. He watched him go till he passed over the crest and disappeared. Then he turned his gaze and slowly took in the circle of the world that remained to him now that Bill was gone.

Near the horizon the sun was smouldering dimly, almost obscured by formless mists and vapors, which gave an impression of mass and density without outline or tangibility. The man pulled out his watch, the while resting his weight on one leg. It was four o'clock, and as the season was near the last of July or first of August,—he did not know the precise date within a week or two,—he knew that the sun roughly marked the northwest. He looked to the south and knew that somewhere beyond those bleak hills lay the Great Bear Lake; also, he knew that in that direction the Arctic Circle cut its forbidding way across the Canadian Barrens. This stream in which he stood was a feeder to the Coppermine River, which in turn flowed north and emptied into Coronation Gulf and the Arctic Ocean. He had never been there, but he had seen it, once, on a Hudson Bay Company chart.

Again his gaze completed the circle of the world about him. It was not a heartening spectacle. Everywhere was soft sky-line. The hills were all low-lying. There were no trees, no shrubs, no grasses—naught but a tremendous and terrible desolation that sent fear swiftly dawning into his eyes.

"Bill!" he whispered, once and twice; "Bill!"

He cowered in the midst of the milky water, as though the vastness were pressing in upon him with overwhelming force, brutally crushing him with its complacent awfulness. He began to shake as with an ague-fit, till the gun fell from his hand with a splash. This served to rouse him. He fought with his fear and pulled himself together, groping in the water and recovering the weapon. He hitched his pack farther over on his left shoulder, so as to take a portion of its weight from off the injured ankle. Then he proceeded, slowly and carefully, wincing with pain, to the bank.

He did not stop. With a desperation that was madness, unmindful of the pain, he hurried up the slope to the crest of the hill over which his comrade had disappeared—more grotesque and comical by far than that limping, jerking comrade. But at the crest he saw a shallow valley, empty of life. He fought with his fear again, overcame it, hitched the pack still farther over on his left shoulder, and lurched on down the slope.

The bottom of the valley was soggy with water, which the thick moss held, spongelike, close to the surface. This water squirted out from under his feet at every step, and each time he lifted a foot the action culminated in a sucking sound as the wet moss reluctantly released its grip. He picked his way from muskeg to muskeg, and followed the other man's footsteps along and across the rocky ledges which thrust like islets through the sea of moss.

Though alone, he was not lost. Farther on he knew he would come to where dead spruce and fir, very small and weazened, bordered the shore of a little lake, the *titchin-nichilie*, in the tongue of the country, the "land of little sticks." And into that lake flowed a small stream, the water of which was not milky. There was rush-grass on that stream— this he remembered well—but no timber, and he would follow it till its first trickle ceased at a divide. He would cross this divide to the first trickle of another stream, flowing to the west, which he would follow until it emptied into the river Dease, and here he would find a cache under an upturned canoe and piled over with many rocks. And in this cache would be ammunition for his empty gun, fish-hooks and lines, a small net—all the utilities for the killing and snaring of food. Also, he would find flour,—not much,—a piece of bacon, and some beans.

Bill would be waiting for him there, and they would paddle away south down the Dease to the Great Bear Lake. And south across the lake they would go, ever south, till they gained the Mackenzie. And south, still south, they would go, while the winter raced vainly after them, and the ice formed in the eddies, and the days grew chill and crisp, south to some warm Hudson Bay Company post, where timber grew tall and generous and there was grub without end.

These were the thoughts of the man as he strove onward. But hard as he strove with his body, he strove equally hard with his mind, trying to think that Bill had not deserted him, that Bill would surely wait for him at the cache. He was compelled to think this thought, or else there would not be any use to strive, and he would have lain down and died. And as the dim ball of the sun sank slowly into the northwest he covered every inch—and many times—of his and Bill's flight south before the downcoming winter. And he conned the grub of the cache and the grub of the Hudson Bay Company post over and over again. He had not eaten for two days; for a far longer time he had not had all he wanted to eat. Often he stooped and picked pale muskeg berries, put them into his mouth, and chewed and swallowed them. A muskeg berry is a bit of seed enclosed in a bit of water. In the mouth the water melts away and the seed chews sharp and bitter. The man knew there was no nourishment in the berries, but he chewed them patiently with a hope greater than knowledge and defying experience.

At nine o'clock he stubbed his toe on a rocky ledge, and from sheer weariness and weakness staggered and fell. He lay for some time, without movement, on his side. Then he slipped out of the pack-straps and clumsily dragged himself into a sitting posture. It was not yet dark, and in the lingering twilight he groped about among the rocks for shreds of dry moss. When he had gathered a heap he built a fire,—a smouldering, smudgy fire,—and put a tin pot of water on to boil.

He unwrapped his pack and the first thing he did was to count his matches. There were sixty-seven. He counted them three times to make sure. He divided them into several portions, wrapping them in oil paper, disposing of one bunch in his empty tobacco pouch, of another bunch in the inside band of his battered hat, of a third bunch under his shirt on the chest. This accomplished, a panic came upon him, and he unwrapped them all and counted them again. There were still sixty-seven.

He dried his wet foot-gear by the fire. The moccasins were in soggy shreds. The blanket socks were worn through in places, and his feet were raw and bleeding. His ankle was throbbing, and he gave it an examination. It had swollen to the size of his knee. He tore a long strip from one of his two blankets and bound the ankle tightly. He tore other strips and bound them about his feet to serve for both moccasins and socks. Then he drank the pot of water, steaming hot, wound his watch, and crawled between his blankets.

He slept like a dead man. The brief darkness around midnight came and went. The sun arose in the northeast—at least the day dawned in that quarter, for the sun was hidden by gray clouds.

At six o'clock he awoke, quietly lying on his back. He gazed straight up into the gray sky and knew that he was hungry. As he rolled over on his elbow he was startled by a loud snort, and saw a bull caribou regarding him with alert curiosity. The animal was not mere than fifty feet away, and instantly into the man's mind leaped the vision and the savor of a caribou steak sizzling and frying over a fire. Mechanically he reached for the empty gun, drew a bead, and pulled the trigger. The bull snorted and leaped away, his hoofs rattling and clattering as he fled across the ledges.

The man cursed and flung the empty gun from him. He groaned aloud as he started to drag himself to his feet. It was a slow and arduous task.

His joints were like rusty hinges. They worked harshly in their sockets, with much friction, and each bending or unbending was accomplished only through a sheer exertion of will. When he finally gained his feet, another minute or so was consumed in straightening up, so that he could stand erect as a man should stand.

He crawled up a small knoll and surveyed the prospect. There were no trees, no bushes, nothing but a gray sea of moss scarcely diversified by gray rocks, gray lakelets, and gray streamlets. The sky was gray. There was no sun nor hint of sun. He had no idea of north, and he had forgotten the way he had come to this spot the night before. But he was not lost. He knew that. Soon he would come to the land of the little sticks. He felt that it lay off to the left somewhere, not far—possibly just over the next low hill.

He went back to put his pack into shape for travelling. He assured himself of the existence of his three separate parcels of matches, though he did not stop to count them. But he did linger, debating, over a squat moose-hide sack. It was not large. He could hide it under his two hands. He knew that it weighed fifteen pounds,—as much as all the rest of the pack,—and it worried him. He finally set it to one side and proceeded to roll the pack. He paused to gaze at the squat moose-hide sack. He picked it up hastily with a defiant glance about him, as though the desolation were trying to rob him of it; and when he rose to his feet to stagger on into the day, it was included in the pack on his back.

He bore away to the left, stopping now and again to eat muskeg berries. His ankle had stiffened, his limp was more pronounced, but the pain of it was as nothing compared with the pain of his stomach. The hunger pangs were sharp. They gnawed and gnawed until he could not keep his mind steady on the course he must pursue to gain the land of little sticks. The muskeg berries did not allay this gnawing, while they made his tongue and the roof of his mouth sore with their irritating bite.

He came upon a valley where rock ptarmigan rose on whirring wings from the ledges and muskegs. Ker—ker—ker was the cry they made. He threw stones at them, but could not hit them. He placed his pack on the ground and stalked them as a cat stalks a sparrow. The sharp rocks cut through his pants' legs till his knees left a trail of blood; but the hurt was lost in the hurt of his hunger. He squirmed over the wet moss, saturating his clothes and chilling his body; but he was not aware of it, so great was his fever for food. And always the ptarmigan rose, whirring, before him, till their ker—ker—ker became a mock to him, and he cursed them and cried aloud at them with their own cry.

Once he crawled upon one that must have been asleep. He did not see it till it shot up in his face from its rocky nook. He made a clutch as startled as was the rise of the ptarmigan, and there remained in his hand three tail-feathers. As he watched its flight he hated it, as though it had done him some terrible wrong. Then he returned and shouldered his pack.

As the day wore along he came into valleys or swales where game was more plentiful. A band of caribou passed by, twenty and odd animals, tantalizingly within rifle range. He felt a wild desire to run after them, a certitude that he could run them down. A black fox came toward him, carrying a ptarmigan in his mouth. The man shouted. It was a fearful cry, but the fox, leaping away in fright, did not drop the ptarmigan.

Late in the afternoon he followed a stream, milky with lime, which ran through sparse patches of rush-grass. Grasping these rushes firmly near the root, he pulled up what resembled a young onion-sprout no larger than a shingle-nail. It was tender, and his teeth sank into it with a crunch that promised deliciously of food. But its fibers were tough. It was composed of stringy filaments saturated with water, like the berries, and devoid of nourishment. He threw off his pack and went into the rush-grass on hands and knees, crunching and munching, like some bovine creature.

He was very weary and often wished to rest—to lie down and sleep; but he was continually driven on—not so much by his desire to gain the land of little sticks as by his hunger. He searched little ponds for frogs and dug up the earth with his nails for worms, though he knew in spite that neither frogs nor worms existed so far north.

He looked into every pool of water vainly, until, as the long twilight came on, he discovered a solitary fish, the size of a minnow, in such a pool. He plunged his arm in up to the shoulder, but it eluded him. He reached for it with both hands and stirred up the milky mud at the bottom. In his excitement he fell in, wetting himself to the waist. Then the water was too muddy to admit of his seeing the fish, and he was compelled to wait until the sediment had settled.

The pursuit was renewed, till the water was again muddied. But he could not wait. He unstrapped the tin bucket and began to bale the pool. He baled wildly at first, splashing himself and flinging the water so short a distance that it ran back into the pool. He worked more carefully, striving to be cool, though his heart was pounding against his chest and his hands were trembling. At the end of half an hour the pool was nearly dry. Not a cupful of water remained. And there was no fish. He found a hidden crevice among the stones through which it had escaped to the adjoining and larger pool—a pool which he could not empty in a night and a day. Had he known of the crevice, he could have closed it with a rock at the beginning and the fish would have been his.

Thus he thought, and crumpled up and sank down upon the wet earth. At first he cried softly to himself, then he cried loudly to the pitiless desolation that ringed him around; and for a long time after he was shaken by great dry sobs.

He built a fire and warmed himself by drinking quarts of hot water, and made camp on a rocky ledge in the same fashion he had the night before. The last thing he did was to see that his matches were dry and to wind his watch. The blankets were wet and clammy. His ankle pulsed with pain. But he knew only that he was hungry, and through his restless sleep he dreamed of feasts and banquets and of food served and spread in all imaginable ways.

He awoke chilled and sick. There was no sun. The gray of earth and sky had become deeper, more profound. A raw wind was blowing, and the first flurries of snow were whitening the hilltops. The air about him thickened and grew white while he made a fire and boiled more water. It was wet snow, half rain, and the flakes were large and soggy. At first they melted as soon as they came in contact with the earth, but ever more fell, covering the ground, putting out the fire, spoiling his supply of moss-fuel.

This was a signal for him to strap on his pack and stumble onward, he knew not where. He was not concerned with the land of little sticks, nor with Bill and the cache under the upturned canoe by the river Dease. He was mastered by the verb "to eat." He was hunger-mad. He took no heed of the course he pursued, so long as that course led him through the swale bottoms. He felt his way through the wet snow to the watery muskeg berries, and went by feel as he pulled up the rush-grass by the roots. But it was tasteless stuff and did not satisfy. He found a weed that tasted sour and he ate all he could find of it, which was not much, for it was a creeping growth, easily hidden under the several inches of snow.

He had no fire that night, nor hot water, and crawled under his blanket to sleep the broken hunger-sleep. The snow turned into a cold rain. He awakened many times to feel it falling on his upturned face. Day came—a gray day and no sun. It had ceased raining. The keenness of his hunger had departed. Sensibility, as far as concerned the yearning for food, had been exhausted. There was a dull, heavy ache in his stomach, but it did not bother him so much. He was more rational, and once more he was chiefly interested in the land of little sticks and the cache by the river Dease.

He ripped the remnant of one of his blankets into strips and bound his bleeding feet. Also, he recinched the injured ankle and prepared himself for a day of travel. When he came to his pack, he paused long over the squat moose-hide sack, but in the end it went with him.

The snow had melted under the rain, and only the hilltops showed white. The sun came out, and he succeeded in locating the points of the compass, though he knew now that he was lost. Perhaps, in his previous days' wanderings, he had edged away too far to the left. He now bore off to the right to counteract the possible deviation from his true course.

Though the hunger pangs were no longer so exquisite, he realized that he was weak. He was compelled to pause for frequent rests, when he attacked the muskeg berries and rush-grass patches. His tongue felt dry and large, as though covered with a fine hairy growth, and it tasted bitter in his mouth. His heart gave him a great deal of trouble. When he had travelled a few minutes it would begin a remorseless thump, thump, thump, and then leap up and away in a painful flutter of beats that choked him and made him go faint and dizzy.

In the middle of the day he found two minnows in a large pool. It was impossible to bale it, but he was calmer now and managed to catch them in his tin bucket. They were no longer than his little finger, but he was not particularly hungry. The dull ache in his stomach had been growing duller and fainter. It seemed almost that his stomach was dozing. He ate the fish raw, masticating with painstaking care, for the eating was an act of pure reason. While he had no desire to eat, he knew that he must eat to live.

In the evening he caught three more minnows, eating two and saving the third for breakfast. The sun had dried stray shreds of moss, and he was able to warm himself with hot water. He had not covered more than ten miles that day; and the next day, travelling whenever his heart permitted him, he covered no more than five miles. But his stomach did not give him the slightest uneasiness. It had gone to sleep. He was in a strange country, too, and the caribou were growing more plentiful, also the wolves. Often their yelps drifted across the desolation, and once he saw three of them slinking away before his path.

Another night; and in the morning, being more rational, he untied the leather string that fastened the squat moose-hide sack. From its open mouth poured a yellow stream of coarse gold-dust and nuggets. He roughly divided the gold in halves, caching one half on a prominent ledge, wrapped in a piece of blanket, and returning the other half to the sack. He also began to use strips of the one remaining blanket for his feet. He still clung to his gun, for there were cartridges in that cache by the river Dease.

This was a day of fog, and this day hunger awoke in him again. He was very weak and was afflicted with a giddiness which at times blinded him. It was no uncommon thing now for him to stumble and fall; and stumbling once, he fell squarely into a ptarmigan nest. There were four newly hatched chicks, a day old—little specks of pulsating life no more than a mouthful; and he ate them ravenously, thrusting them alive into his mouth and crunching them like egg-shells between his teeth. The mother ptarmigan beat about him with great outcry. He used his gun as a club with which to knock her over, but she dodged out of reach. He threw stones at her and with one chance shot broke a wing. Then she fluttered away, running, trailing the broken wing, with him in pursuit.

The little chicks had no more than whetted his appetite. He hopped and bobbed clumsily along on his injured ankle, throwing stones and screaming hoarsely at times; at other times hopping and bobbing silently along, picking himself up grimly and patiently when he fell, or rubbing his eyes with his hand when the giddiness threatened to overpower him.

The chase led him across swampy ground in the bottom of the valley, and he came upon footprints in the soggy moss. They were not his own—he could see that. They must be Bill's. But he could not stop, for the mother ptarmigan was running on. He would catch her first, then he would return and investigate.

He exhausted the mother ptarmigan; but he exhausted himself. She lay panting on her side. He lay panting on his side, a dozen feet away, unable to crawl to her. And as he recovered she recovered, fluttering out of reach as his hungry hand went out to her. The chase was resumed. Night settled down and she escaped. He stumbled from weakness and pitched head foremost on his face, cutting his cheek, his pack upon his back. He did not move for a long while; then he rolled over on his side, wound his watch, and lay there until morning.

Another day of fog. Half of his last blanket had gone into foot-wrappings. He failed to pick up Bill's trail. It did not matter. His hunger was driving him too compellingly—only—only he wondered if Bill, too, were lost. By midday the irk of his pack became too oppressive. Again he divided the gold, this time merely spilling half of it on the ground. In the afternoon he threw the rest of it away, there remaining to him only the half-blanket, the tin bucket, and the rifle.

An hallucination began to trouble him. He felt confident that one cartridge remained to him. It was in the chamber of the rifle and he had overlooked it. On the other hand, he knew all the time that the chamber was empty. But the hallucination persisted. He fought it off for hours, then threw his rifle open and was confronted with emptiness. The disappointment was as bitter as though he had really expected to find the cartridge.

He plodded on for half an hour, when the hallucination arose again. Again he fought it, and still it persisted, till for very relief he opened his rifle to unconvince himself. At times his mind wandered farther afield, and he plodded on, a mere automaton, strange conceits and whimsicalities gnawing at his brain like worms. But these excursions out of the real were of brief duration, for ever the pangs of the hunger-bite called him back. He was jerked back abruptly once from such an excursion by a sight that caused him nearly to faint. He reeled and swayed, doddering like a drunken man to keep from falling. Before him stood a horse. A horse! He could not believe his eyes. A thick mist was in them, intershot with sparkling points of light. He rubbed his eyes savagely to clear his vision, and beheld, not a horse, but a great brown bear. The animal was studying him with bellicose curiosity.

The man had brought his gun halfway to his shoulder before he realized. He lowered it and drew his hunting-knife from its beaded sheath at his hip. Before him was meat and life. He ran his thumb along the edge of his knife. It was sharp. The point was sharp. He would fling himself upon the bear and kill it. But his heart began its warning thump, thump, thump. Then followed the wild upward leap and tattoo of flutters, the pressing as of an iron band about his forehead, the creeping of the dizziness into his brain.

His desperate courage was evicted by a great surge of fear. In his weakness, what if the animal attacked him? He drew himself up to his most imposing stature, gripping the knife and staring hard at the bear. The bear advanced clumsily a couple of steps, reared up, and gave vent to a tentative growl. If the man ran, he would run after him; but the man did not run. He was animated now with the courage of fear. He, too, growled, savagely, terribly, voicing the fear that is to life germane and that lies twisted about life's deepest roots.

The bear edged away to one side, growling menacingly, himself appalled by this mysterious creature that appeared upright and unafraid. But the man did not move. He stood like a statue till the danger was past, when he yielded to a fit of trembling and sank down into the wet moss.

He pulled himself together and went on, afraid now in a new way. It was not the fear that he should die passively from lack of food, but that he should be destroyed violently before starvation had exhausted the last particle of the endeavor in him that made toward surviving. There were the wolves. Back and forth across the desolation drifted their howls, weaving the very air into a fabric of menace that was so tangible that he found himself, arms in the air, pressing it back from him as it might be the walls of a wind-blown tent.

Now and again the wolves, in packs of two and three, crossed his path. But they sheered clear of him. They were not in sufficient numbers, and besides they were hunting the caribou, which did not battle, while this strange creature that walked erect might scratch and bite.

In the late afternoon he came upon scattered bones where the wolves had made a kill. The debris had been a caribou calf an hour before, squawking and running and very much alive. He contemplated the bones, clean-picked and polished, pink with the cell-life in them which had not yet died. Could it possibly be that he might be that ere the day was done! Such was life, eh? A vain and fleeting thing. It was only life that pained. There was no hurt in death. To die was to sleep. It meant cessation, rest. Then why was he not content to die?

But he did not moralize long. He was squatting in the moss, a bone in his mouth, sucking at the shreds of life that still dyed it faintly pink. The sweet meaty taste, thin and elusive almost as a memory, maddened him. He closed his jaws on the bones and crunched. Sometimes it was the bone that broke, sometimes his teeth. Then he crushed the bones between rocks, pounded them to a pulp, and swallowed them. He pounded his fingers, too, in his haste, and yet found a moment in which to feel surprise at the fact that his fingers did not hurt much when caught under the descending rock.

Came frightful days of snow and rain. He did not know when he made camp, when he broke camp. He travelled in the night as much as in the day. He rested wherever he fell, crawled on whenever the dying life in him flickered up and burned less dimly. He, as a man, no longer strove. It was the life in him, unwilling to die, that drove him on. He did not suffer. His nerves had become blunted, numb, while his mind was filled with weird visions and delicious dreams.

But ever he sucked and chewed on the crushed bones of the caribou calf, the least remnants of which he had gathered up and carried with him. He crossed no more hills or divides, but automatically followed a large stream which flowed through a wide and shallow valley. He did not see this stream nor this valley. He saw nothing save visions. Soul and body walked or crawled side by side, yet apart, so slender was the thread that bound them.

He awoke in his right mind, lying on his back on a rocky ledge. The sun was shining bright and warm. Afar off he heard the squawking of caribou calves. He was aware of vague memories of rain and wind and snow, but whether he had been beaten by the storm for two days or two weeks he did not know.

For some time he lay without movement, the genial sunshine pouring upon him and saturating his miserable body with its warmth. A fine day, he thought. Perhaps he could manage to locate himself. By a painful effort he rolled over on his side. Below him flowed a wide and sluggish river. Its unfamiliarity puzzled him. Slowly he followed it with his eyes, winding in wide sweeps among the bleak, bare hills, bleaker and barer and lower-lying than any hills he had yet encountered. Slowly, deliberately, without excitement or more than the most casual interest, he followed the course of the strange stream toward the sky-line and saw it emptying into a bright and shining sea. He was still unexcited. Most unusual, he thought, a vision or a mirage—more likely a vision, a trick of his disordered mind. He was confirmed in this by sight of a ship lying at anchor in the midst of the shining sea. He closed his eyes for a while, then opened them. Strange how the vision persisted! Yet not strange. He knew there were no seas or ships in the heart of the barren lands, just as he had known there was no cartridge in the empty rifle.

He heard a snuffle behind him—a half-choking gasp or cough. Very slowly, because of his exceeding weakness and stiffness, he rolled over on his other side. He could see nothing near at hand, but he waited patiently. Again came the snuffle and cough, and outlined between two jagged rocks not a score of feet away he made out the gray head of a wolf. The sharp ears were not pricked so sharply as he had seen them on other wolves; the eyes were bleared and bloodshot, the head seemed to droop limply and forlornly. The animal blinked continually in the sunshine. It seemed sick. As he looked it snuffled and coughed again.

This, at least, was real, he thought, and turned on the other side so that he might see the reality of the world which had been veiled from him before by the vision. But the sea still shone in the distance and the ship was plainly discernible. Was it reality, after all? He closed his eyes for a long while and thought, and then it came to him. He had been making north by east, away from the Dease Divide and into the Coppermine Valley. This wide and sluggish river was the Coppermine. That shining sea was the Arctic Ocean. That ship was a whaler, strayed east, far east, from the mouth of the Mackenzie, and it was lying at anchor in Coronation Gulf. He remembered the Hudson Bay Company chart he had seen long ago, and it was all clear and reasonable to him.

He sat up and turned his attention to immediate affairs. He had worn through the blanket-wrappings, and his feet were shapeless lumps of raw meat. His last blanket was gone. Rifle and knife were both missing. He had lost his hat somewhere, with the bunch of matches in the band, but the matches against his chest were safe and dry inside the tobacco pouch and oil paper. He looked at his watch. It marked eleven o'clock and was still running. Evidently he had kept it wound.

He was calm and collected. Though extremely weak, he had no sensation of pain. He was not hungry. The thought of food was not even pleasant to him, and whatever he did was done by his reason alone. He ripped off his pants' legs to the knees and bound them about his feet. Somehow he had succeeded in retaining the tin bucket. He would have some hot water before he began what he foresaw was to be a terrible journey to the ship.

His movements were slow. He shook as with a palsy. When he started to collect dry moss, he found he could not rise to his feet. He tried again and again, then contented himself with crawling about on hands and knees. Once he crawled near to the sick wolf. The animal dragged itself reluctantly out of his way, licking its chops with a tongue which seemed hardly to have the strength to curl. The man noticed that the tongue was not the customary healthy red. It was a yellowish brown and seemed coated with a rough and half-dry mucus.

After he had drunk a quart of hot water the man found he was able to stand, and even to walk as well as a dying man might be supposed to walk. Every minute or so he was compelled to rest. His steps were feeble and uncertain, just as the wolf's that trailed him were feeble and uncertain; and that night, when the shining sea was blotted out by blackness, he knew he was nearer to it by no more than four miles.

Throughout the night he heard the cough of the sick wolf, and now and then the squawking of the caribou calves. There was life all around him, but it was strong life, very much alive and well, and he knew the sick wolf clung to the sick man's trail in the hope that the man would die first. In the morning, on opening his eyes, he beheld it regarding him with a wistful and hungry stare. It stood crouched, with tail between its legs, like a miserable and woe-begone dog. It shivered in the chill morning wind, and grinned dispiritedly when the man spoke to it in a voice that achieved no more than a hoarse whisper.

The sun rose brightly, and all morning the man tottered and fell toward the ship on the shining sea. The weather was perfect. It was the brief Indian Summer of the high latitudes. It might last a week. To-morrow or next day it might he gone.

In the afternoon the man came upon a trail. It was of another man, who did not walk, but who dragged himself on all fours. The man thought it might be Bill, but he thought in a dull, uninterested way. He had no curiosity. In fact, sensation and emotion had left him. He was no longer susceptible to pain. Stomach and nerves had gone to sleep. Yet the life that was in him drove him on. He was very weary, but it refused to die. It was because it refused to die that he still ate muskeg berries and minnows, drank his hot water, and kept a wary eye on the sick wolf.

He followed the trail of the other man who dragged himself along, and soon came to the end of it—a few fresh-picked bones where the soggy moss was marked by the foot-pads of many wolves. He saw a squat moose-hide sack, mate to his own, which had been torn by sharp teeth. He picked it up, though its weight was almost too much for his feeble fingers. Bill had carried it to the last. Ha! ha! He would have the laugh on Bill. He would survive and carry it to the ship in the shining sea. His mirth was hoarse and ghastly, like a raven's croak, and the sick wolf joined him, howling lugubriously. The man ceased suddenly. How could he have the laugh on Bill if that were Bill; if those bones, so pinky-white and clean, were Bill?

He turned away. Well, Bill had deserted him; but he would not take the gold, nor would he suck Bill's bones. Bill would have, though, had it been the other way around, he mused as he staggered on.

He came to a pool of water. Stooping over in quest of minnows, he jerked his head back as though he had been stung. He had caught sight of his reflected face. So horrible was it that sensibility awoke long enough to be shocked. There were three minnows in the pool, which was too large to drain; and after several ineffectual attempts to catch them in the tin bucket he forbore. He was afraid, because of his great weakness, that he might fall in and drown. It was for this reason that he did not trust himself to the river astride one of the many drift-logs which lined its sand-spits.

That day he decreased the distance between him and the ship by three miles; the next day by two—for he was crawling now as Bill had crawled; and the end of the fifth day found the ship still seven miles away and him unable to make even a mile a day. Still the Indian Summer held on, and he continued to crawl and faint, turn and turn about; and ever the sick wolf coughed and wheezed at his heels. His knees had become raw meat like his feet, and though he padded them with the shirt from his back it was a red track he left behind him on the moss and stones. Once, glancing back, he saw the wolf licking hungrily his bleeding trail, and he saw sharply what his own end might be—unless—unless he could get the wolf. Then began as grim a tragedy of existence as was ever played—a sick man that crawled, a sick wolf that limped, two creatures dragging their dying carcasses across the desolation and hunting each other's lives.

Had it been a well wolf, it would not have mattered so much to the man; but the thought of going to feed the maw of that loathsome and all but dead thing was repugnant to him. He was finicky. His mind had begun to wander again, and to be perplexed by hallucinations, while his lucid intervals grew rarer and shorter.

He was awakened once from a faint by a wheeze close in his ear. The wolf leaped lamely back, losing its footing and falling in its weakness. It was ludicrous, but he was not amused. Nor was he even afraid. He was too far gone for that. But his mind was for the moment clear, and he lay and considered. The ship was no more than four miles away. He could see it quite distinctly when he rubbed the mists out of his eyes, and he could see the white sail of a small boat cutting the water of the shining sea. But he could never crawl those four miles. He knew that, and was very calm in the knowledge. He knew that he could not crawl half a mile. And yet he wanted to live. It was unreasonable that he should die after all he had undergone. Fate asked too much of him. And, dying, he declined to die. It was stark madness, perhaps, but in the very grip of Death he defied Death and refused to die.

He closed his eyes and composed himself with infinite precaution. He steeled himself to keep above the suffocating languor that lapped like a rising tide through all the wells of his being. It was very like a sea, this deadly languor, that rose and rose and drowned his consciousness bit by bit. Sometimes he was all but submerged, swimming through oblivion with a faltering stroke; and again, by some strange alchemy of soul, he would find another shred of will and strike out more strongly.

Without movement he lay on his back, and he could hear, slowly drawing near and nearer, the wheezing intake and output of the sick wolf's breath. It drew closer, ever closer, through an infinitude of time, and he did not move. It was at his ear. The harsh dry tongue grated like sandpaper against his cheek. His hands shot out—or at least he willed them to shoot out. The fingers were curved like talons, but they closed on empty air. Swiftness and certitude require strength, and the man had not this strength.

The patience of the wolf was terrible. The man's patience was no less terrible. For half a day he lay motionless, fighting off unconsciousness and waiting for the thing that was to feed upon him and upon which he wished to feed. Sometimes the languid sea rose over him and he dreamed long dreams; but ever through it all, waking and dreaming, he waited for the wheezing breath and the harsh caress of the tongue.

He did not hear the breath, and he slipped slowly from some dream to the feel of the tongue along his hand. He waited. The fangs pressed softly; the pressure increased; the wolf was exerting its last strength in an effort to sink teeth in the food for which it had waited so long. But the man had waited long, and the lacerated hand closed on the jaw. Slowly, while the wolf struggled feebly and the hand clutched feebly, the other hand crept across to a grip. Five minutes later the whole weight of the man's body was on top of the wolf. The hands had not sufficient strength to choke the wolf, but the face of the man was pressed close to the throat of the wolf and the mouth of the man was full of hair. At the end of half an hour the man was aware of a warm trickle in his throat. It was not pleasant. It was like molten lead being forced into his stomach, and it was forced by his will alone. Later the man rolled over on his back and slept.

THERE WERE SOME MEMBERS OF a scientific expedition on the whale-ship *Bedford*. From the deck they remarked a strange object on the shore. It was moving down the beach toward the water. They were unable to classify it, and, being scientific men, they climbed into the whale-boat alongside and went ashore to see. And they saw something that was alive but which could hardly be called a man. It was blind, unconscious. It squirmed along the ground like some monstrous worm. Most of its efforts were ineffectual, but it was persistent, and it writhed and twisted and went ahead perhaps a score of feet an hour.

THREE WEEKS AFTERWARD THE MAN lay in a bunk on the whale-ship *Bedford*, and with tears streaming down his wasted cheeks told who he was and what he had undergone. He also babbled incoherently of his mother, of sunny Southern California, and a home among the orange groves and flowers.

The days were not many after that when he sat at table with the scientific men and ship's officers. He gloated over the spectacle of so much food, watching it anxiously as it went into the mouths of others. With the disappearance of each mouthful an expression of deep regret came into his eyes. He was quite sane, yet he hated those men at mealtime. He was haunted by a fear that the food would not last. He inquired of the cook, the cabin-boy, the captain, concerning the food stores. They reassured him countless times; but he could not believe them, and pried cunningly about the lazarette to see with his own eyes.

It was noticed that the man was getting fat. He grew stouter with each day. The scientific men shook their heads and theorized. They limited the man at his meals, but still his girth increased and he swelled prodigiously under his shirt.

The sailors grinned. They knew. And when the scientific men set a watch on the man, they knew too. They saw him slouch for'ard after breakfast, and, like a mendicant, with outstretched palm, accost a sailor. The sailor grinned and passed him a fragment of sea biscuit. He clutched it avariciously, looked at it as a miser looks at gold, and thrust it into his shirt bosom. Similar were the donations from other grinning sailors.

The scientific men were discreet. They let him alone. But they privily examined his bunk. It was lined with hardtack; the mattress was stuffed with hardtack; every nook and cranny was filled with hardtack. Yet he was sane. He was taking precautions against another possible famine—that was all. He would recover from it, the scientific men said; and he did, ere the *Bedford's* anchor rumbled down in San Francisco Bay.

# A Day's Lodging

*It was the gosh-dangdest stampede I ever seen. A thousand
dog-teams hittin' the ice. You couldn't see 'm fer smoke. Two white
men an' a Swede froze to death that night, an' there was a dozen
busted their lungs. But didn't I see with my own eyes the bottom
of the water-hole? It was yellow with gold like a mustard-plaster.
That's why I staked the Yukon for a minin' claim. That's what made
the stampede. An' then there was nothin' to it. That's what I said—
nothin' to it. An' I ain't got over guessin' yet.*

—Narrative of Shorty

John Messner clung with mittened hand to the bucking gee-pole and
held the sled in the trail. With the other mittened hand he rubbed
his cheeks and nose. He rubbed his cheeks and nose every little while.
In point of fact, he rarely ceased from rubbing them, and sometimes, as
their numbness increased, he rubbed fiercely. His forehead was covered
by the visor of his fur cap, the flaps of which went over his ears. The
rest of his face was protected by a thick beard, golden-brown under its
coating of frost.

Behind him churned a heavily loaded Yukon sled, and before him
toiled a string of five dogs. The rope by which they dragged the sled
rubbed against the side of Messner's leg. When the dogs swung on
a bend in the trail, he stepped over the rope. There were many bends,
and he was compelled to step over it often. Sometimes he tripped on
the rope, or stumbled, and at all times he was awkward, betraying a
weariness so great that the sled now and again ran upon his heels.

When he came to a straight piece of trail, where the sled could
get along for a moment without guidance, he let go the gee-pole
and batted his right hand sharply upon the hard wood. He found it
difficult to keep up the circulation in that hand. But while he pounded
the one hand, he never ceased from rubbing his nose and cheeks with
the other.

"It's too cold to travel, anyway," he said. He spoke aloud, after the
manner of men who are much by themselves. "Only a fool would travel
at such a temperature. If it isn't eighty below, it's because it's seventy-
nine."

He pulled out his watch, and after some fumbling got it back into the breast pocket of his thick woollen jacket. Then he surveyed the heavens and ran his eye along the white sky-line to the south.

"Twelve o'clock," he mumbled, "A clear sky, and no sun."

He plodded on silently for ten minutes, and then, as though there had been no lapse in his speech, he added:

"And no ground covered, and it's too cold to travel."

Suddenly he yelled "Whoa!" at the dogs, and stopped. He seemed in a wild panic over his right hand, and proceeded to hammer it furiously against the gee-pole.

"You—poor—devils!" he addressed the dogs, which had dropped down heavily on the ice to rest. His was a broken, jerky utterance, caused by the violence with which he hammered his numb hand upon the wood. "What have you done anyway that a two-legged other animal should come along, break you to harness, curb all your natural proclivities, and make slave-beasts out of you?"

He rubbed his nose, not reflectively, but savagely, in order to drive the blood into it, and urged the dogs to their work again. He travelled on the frozen surface of a great river. Behind him it stretched away in a mighty curve of many miles, losing itself in a fantastic jumble of mountains, snow-covered and silent. Ahead of him the river split into many channels to accommodate the freight of islands it carried on its breast. These islands were silent and white. No animals nor humming insects broke the silence. No birds flew in the chill air. There was no sound of man, no mark of the handiwork of man. The world slept, and it was like the sleep of death.

John Messner seemed succumbing to the apathy of it all. The frost was benumbing his spirit. He plodded on with bowed head, unobservant, mechanically rubbing nose and cheeks, and batting his steering hand against the gee-pole in the straight trail-stretches.

But the dogs were observant, and suddenly they stopped, turning their heads and looking back at their master out of eyes that were wistful and questioning. Their eyelashes were frosted white, as were their muzzles, and they had all the seeming of decrepit old age, what of the frost-rime and exhaustion.

The man was about to urge them on, when he checked himself, roused up with an effort, and looked around. The dogs had stopped beside a water-hole, not a fissure, but a hole man-made, chopped laboriously with an axe through three and a half feet of ice. A thick skin of new ice showed that it had not been used for some time. Messner glanced about him. The dogs were already pointing the way, each wistful and hoary muzzle turned toward the dim snow-path that left the main river trail and climbed the bank of the island.

"All right, you sore-footed brutes," he said. "I'll investigate. You're not a bit more anxious to quit than I am."

He climbed the bank and disappeared. The dogs did not lie down, but on their feet eagerly waited his return. He came back to them, took a hauling-rope from the front of the sled, and put it around his shoulders. Then he *gee'd* the dogs to the right and put them at the bank on the run. It was a stiff pull, but their weariness fell from them as they crouched low to the snow, whining with eagerness and gladness as they struggled upward to the last ounce of effort in their bodies. When a dog slipped or faltered, the one behind nipped his hind quarters. The man shouted encouragement and threats, and threw all his weight on the hauling-rope.

They cleared the bank with a rush, swung to the left, and dashed up to a small log cabin. It was a deserted cabin of a single room, eight feet by ten on the inside. Messner unharnessed the animals, unloaded his sled and took possession. The last chance wayfarer had left a supply of firewood. Messner set up his light sheet-iron stove and starred a fire. He put five sun-cured salmon into the oven to thaw out for the dogs, and from the water-hole filled his coffee-pot and cooking-pail.

While waiting for the water to boil, he held his face over the stove. The moisture from his breath had collected on his beard and frozen into a great mass of ice, and this he proceeded to thaw out. As it melted and dropped upon the stove it sizzled and rose about him in steam. He helped the process with his fingers, working loose small ice-chunks that fell rattling to the floor.

A wild outcry from the dogs without did not take him from his task. He heard the wolfish snarling and yelping of strange dogs and the sound of voices. A knock came on the door.

"Come in," Messner called, in a voice muffled because at the moment he was sucking loose a fragment of ice from its anchorage on his upper lip.

The door opened, and, gazing out of his cloud of steam, he saw a man and a woman pausing on the threshold.

"Come in," he said peremptorily, "and shut the door!"

Peering through the steam, he could make out but little of their personal appearance. The nose and cheek strap worn by the woman and the trail-wrappings about her head allowed only a pair of black eyes to be seen. The man was dark-eyed and smooth-shaven all except his mustache, which was so iced up as to hide his mouth.

"We just wanted to know if there is any other cabin around here," he said, at the same time glancing over the unfurnished state of the room. "We thought this cabin was empty."

"It isn't my cabin," Messner answered. "I just found it a few minutes ago. Come right in and camp. Plenty of room, and you won't need your stove. There's room for all."

At the sound of his voice the woman peered at him with quick curiousness.

"Get your things off," her companion said to her. "I'll unhitch and get the water so we can start cooking."

Messner took the thawed salmon outside and fed his dogs. He had to guard them against the second team of dogs, and when he had reentered the cabin the other man had unpacked the sled and fetched water. Messner's pot was boiling. He threw in the coffee, settled it with half a cup of cold water, and took the pot from the stove. He thawed some sour-dough biscuits in the oven, at the same time heating a pot of beans he had boiled the night before and that had ridden frozen on the sled all morning.

Removing his utensils from the stove, so as to give the newcomers a chance to cook, he proceeded to take his meal from the top of his grub-box, himself sitting on his bed-roll. Between mouthfuls he talked trail and dogs with the man, who, with head over the stove, was thawing the ice from his mustache. There were two bunks in the cabin, and into one of them, when he had cleared his lip, the stranger tossed his bed-roll.

"We'll sleep here," he said, "unless you prefer this bunk. You're the first comer and you have first choice, you know."

"That's all right," Messner answered. "One bunk's just as good as the other."

He spread his own bedding in the second bunk, and sat down on the edge. The stranger thrust a physician's small travelling case under his blankets at one end to serve for a pillow.

"Doctor?" Messner asked.

"Yes," came the answer, "but I assure you I didn't come into the Klondike to practise."

The woman busied herself with cooking, while the man sliced bacon and fired the stove. The light in the cabin was dim, filtering through in a small window made of onion-skin writing paper and oiled with bacon grease, so that John Messner could not make out very well what the woman looked like. Not that he tried. He seemed to have no interest in her. But she glanced curiously from time to time into the dark corner where he sat.

"Oh, it's a great life," the doctor proclaimed enthusiastically, pausing from sharpening his knife on the stovepipe. "What I like about it is the struggle, the endeavor with one's own hands, the primitiveness of it, the realness."

"The temperature is real enough," Messner laughed.

"Do you know how cold it actually is?" the doctor demanded.

The other shook his head.

"Well, I'll tell you. Seventy-four below zero by spirit thermometer on the sled."

"That's one hundred and six below freezing point—too cold for travelling, eh?"

"Practically suicide," was the doctor's verdict. "One exerts himself. He breathes heavily, taking into his lungs the frost itself. It chills his lungs, freezes the edges of the tissues. He gets a dry, hacking cough as the dead tissue sloughs away, and dies the following summer of pneumonia, wondering what it's all about. I'll stay in this cabin for a week, unless the thermometer rises at least to fifty below."

"I say, Tess," he said, the next moment, "don't you think that coffee's boiled long enough!"

At the sound of the woman's name, John Messner became suddenly alert. He looked at her quickly, while across his face shot a haunting expression, the ghost of some buried misery achieving swift resurrection. But the next moment, and by an effort of will, the ghost was laid again. His face was as placid as before, though he was still alert, dissatisfied with what the feeble light had shown him of the woman's face.

Automatically, her first act had been to set the coffee-pot back. It was not until she had done this that she glanced at Messner. But already he had composed himself. She saw only a man sitting on the edge of the bunk and incuriously studying the toes of his moccasins. But, as she turned casually to go about her cooking, he shot another swift look at her, and she, glancing as swiftly back, caught his look. He shifted on past her to the doctor, though the slightest smile curled his lip in appreciation of the way she had trapped him.

She drew a candle from the grub-box and lighted it. One look at her illuminated face was enough for Messner. In the small cabin the widest limit was only a matter of several steps, and the next moment she was alongside of him. She deliberately held the candle close to his face and stared at him out of eyes wide with fear and recognition. He smiled quietly back at her.

"What are you looking for, Tess?" the doctor called.

"Hairpins," she replied, passing on and rummaging in a clothes-bag on the bunk.

They served their meal on their grub-box, sitting on Messner's grub-box and facing him. He had stretched out on his bunk to rest, lying on his side, his head on his arm. In the close quarters it was as though the three were together at table.

"What part of the States do you come from?" Messner asked.

"San Francisco," answered the doctor. "I've been in here two years, though."

"I hail from California myself," was Messner's announcement.

The woman looked at him appealingly, but he smiled and went on: "Berkeley, you know."

The other man was becoming interested.

"U. C.?" he asked.

"Yes, Class of '86."

"I meant faculty," the doctor explained. "You remind me of the type."

"Sorry to hear you say so," Messner smiled back. "I'd prefer being taken for a prospector or a dog-musher."

"I don't think he looks any more like a professor than you do a doctor," the woman broke in.

"Thank you," said Messner. Then, turning to her companion, "By the way, Doctor, what is your name, if I may ask?"

"Haythorne, if you'll take my word for it. I gave up cards with civilization."

"And Mrs. Haythorne," Messner smiled and bowed.

She flashed a look at him that was more anger than appeal.

Haythorne was about to ask the other's name. His mouth opened to form the question when Messner cut him off.

"Come to think of it, Doctor, you may possibly be able to satisfy my curiosity. There was a sort of scandal in faculty circles some two or three years ago. The wife of one of the English professors—er, if you will pardon me, Mrs. Haythorne—disappeared with some San Francisco doctor, I understood, though his name does not just now come to my lips. Do you remember the incident?"

Haythorne nodded his head. "Made quite a stir at the time. His name was Womble—Graham Womble. He had a magnificent practice. I knew him somewhat."

"Well, what I was trying to get at was what had become of them. I was wondering if you had heard. They left no trace, hide nor hair."

"He covered his tracks cunningly." Haythorne cleared his throat. "There was rumor that they went to the South Seas—were lost on a trading schooner in a typhoon, or something like that."

"I never heard that," Messner said. "You remember the case, Mrs. Haythorne?"

"Perfectly," she answered, in a voice the control of which was in amazing contrast to the anger that blazed in the face she turned aside so that Haythorne might not see.

The latter was again on the verge of asking his name, when Messner remarked:

"This Dr. Womble, I've heard he was very handsome, and—er—quite a success, so to say, with the ladies."

"Well, if he was, he finished himself off by that affair," Haythorne grumbled.

"And the woman was a termagant—at least so I've been told. It was generally accepted in Berkeley that she made life—er—not exactly paradise for her husband."

"I never heard that," Haythorne rejoined. "In San Francisco the talk was all the other way."

"Woman sort of a martyr, eh?—crucified on the cross of matrimony?"

The doctor nodded. Messner's gray eyes were mildly curious as he went on:

"That was to be expected—two sides to the shield. Living in Berkeley I only got the one side. She was a great deal in San Francisco, it seems."

"Some coffee, please," Haythorne said.

The woman refilled his mug, at the same time breaking into light laughter.

"You're gossiping like a pair of beldames," she chided them.

"It's so interesting," Messner smiled at her, then returned to the doctor. "The husband seems then to have had a not very savory reputation in San Francisco?"

"On the contrary, he was a moral prig," Haythorne blurted out, with apparently undue warmth. "He was a little scholastic shrimp without a drop of red blood in his body."

"Did you know him?"

"Never laid eyes on him. I never knocked about in university circles."

"One side of the shield again," Messner said, with an air of weighing the matter judicially. "While he did not amount to much, it is true—that is, physically—I'd hardly say he was as bad as all that. He did take an active interest in student athletics. And he had some talent. He once wrote a Nativity play that brought him quite a bit of local appreciation. I have heard, also, that he was slated for the head of the English department, only the affair happened and he resigned and went away. It quite broke his career, or so it seemed. At any rate, on our side the shield, it was considered a knock-out blow to him. It was thought he cared a great deal for his wife."

Haythorne, finishing his mug of coffee, grunted uninterestedly and lighted his pipe.

"It was fortunate they had no children," Messner continued.

But Haythorne, with a glance at the stove, pulled on his cap and mittens.

"I'm going out to get some wood," he said. "Then I can take off my moccasins and he comfortable."

The door slammed behind him. For a long minute there was silence. The man continued in the same position on the bed. The woman sat on the grub-box, facing him.

"What are you going to do?" she asked abruptly.

Messner looked at her with lazy indecision. "What do you think I ought to do? Nothing scenic, I hope. You see I am stiff and trail-sore, and this bunk is so restful."

She gnawed her lower lip and fumed dumbly.

"But—" she began vehemently, then clenched her hands and stopped.

"I hope you don't want me to kill Mr.—er—Haythorne," he said gently, almost pleadingly. "It would be most distressing, and, I assure you, really it is unnecessary."

"But you must do something," she cried.

"On the contrary, it is quite conceivable that I do not have to do anything."

"You would stay here?"

He nodded.

She glanced desperately around the cabin and at the bed unrolled on the other bunk. "Night is coming on. You can't stop here. You can't! I tell you, you simply can't!"

"Of course I can. I might remind you that I found this cabin first and that you are my guests."

Again her eyes travelled around the room, and the terror in them leaped up at sight of the other bunk.

"Then we'll have to go," she announced decisively.

"Impossible. You have a dry, hacking cough—the sort Mr.—er—Haythorne so aptly described. You've already slightly chilled your lungs. Besides, he is a physician and knows. He would never permit it."

"Then what are you going to do?" she demanded again, with a tense, quiet utterance that boded an outbreak.

Messner regarded her in a way that was almost paternal, what of the profundity of pity and patience with which he contrived to suffuse it.

"My dear Theresa, as I told you before, I don't know. I really haven't thought about it."

"Oh! You drive me mad!" She sprang to her feet, wringing her hands in impotent wrath. "You never used to be this way."

"I used to be all softness and gentleness," he nodded concurrence. "Was that why you left me?"

"You are so different, so dreadfully calm. You frighten me. I feel you have something terrible planned all the while. But whatever you do, don't do anything rash. Don't get excited—"

"I don't get excited any more," he interrupted. "Not since you went away."

"You have improved—remarkably," she retorted.

He smiled acknowledgment. "While I am thinking about what I shall do, I'll tell you what you will have to do—tell Mr.—er—Haythorne who I am. It may make our stay in this cabin more—may I say, sociable?"

"Why have you followed me into this frightful country?" she asked irrelevantly.

"Don't think I came here looking for you, Theresa. Your vanity shall not be tickled by any such misapprehension. Our meeting is wholly fortuitous. I broke with the life academic and I had to go somewhere. To be honest, I came into the Klondike because I thought it the place you were least liable to be in."

There was a fumbling at the latch, then the door swung in and Haythorne entered with an armful of firewood. At the first warning, Theresa began casually to clear away the dishes. Haythorne went out again after more wood.

"Why didn't you introduce us?" Messner queried.

"I'll tell him," she replied, with a toss of her head. "Don't think I'm afraid."

"I never knew you to be afraid, very much, of anything."

"And I'm not afraid of confession, either," she said, with softening face and voice.

"In your case, I fear, confession is exploitation by indirection, profit-making by ruse, self-aggrandizement at the expense of God."

"Don't be literary," she pouted, with growing tenderness. "I never did like epigrammatic discussion. Besides, I'm not afraid to ask you to forgive me."

"There is nothing to forgive, Theresa. I really should thank you. True, at first I suffered; and then, with all the graciousness of spring, it dawned upon me that I was happy, very happy. It was a most amazing discovery."

"But what if I should return to you?" she asked.

"I should" (he looked at her whimsically), "be greatly perturbed."

"I am your wife. You know you have never got a divorce."

"I see," he meditated. "I have been careless. It will be one of the first things I attend to."

She came over to his side, resting her hand on his arm. "You don't want me, John?" Her voice was soft and caressing, her hand rested like a lure. "If I told you I had made a mistake? If I told you that I was very unhappy?—and I am. And I did make a mistake."

Fear began to grow on Messner. He felt himself wilting under the lightly laid hand. The situation was slipping away from him, all his beautiful calmness was going. She looked at him with melting eyes, and he, too, seemed all dew and melting. He felt himself on the edge of an abyss, powerless to withstand the force that was drawing him over.

"I am coming back to you, John. I am coming back to-day. . . now."

As in a nightmare, he strove under the hand. While she talked, he seemed to hear, rippling softly, the song of the Lorelei. It was as though, somewhere, a piano were playing and the actual notes were impinging on his ear-drums.

Suddenly he sprang to his feet, thrust her from him as her arms attempted to clasp him, and retreated backward to the door. He was in a panic.

"I'll do something desperate!" he cried.

"I warned you not to get excited." She laughed mockingly, and went about washing the dishes. "Nobody wants you. I was just playing with you. I am happier where I am."

But Messner did not believe. He remembered her facility in changing front. She had changed front now. It was exploitation by indirection. She was not happy with the other man. She had discovered her mistake. The flame of his ego flared up at the thought. She wanted to come back to him, which was the one thing he did not want. Unwittingly, his hand rattled the door-latch.

"Don't run away," she laughed. "I won't bite you."

"I am not running away," he replied with child-like defiance, at the same time pulling on his mittens. "I'm only going to get some water."

He gathered the empty pails and cooking pots together and opened the door. He looked back at her.

"Don't forget you're to tell Mr.—er—Haythorne who I am."

Messner broke the skin that had formed on the water-hole within the hour, and filled his pails. But he did not return immediately to the cabin. Leaving the pails standing in the trail, he walked up and down, rapidly, to keep from freezing, for the frost bit into the flesh like fire. His beard was white with his frozen breath when the perplexed and frowning brows relaxed and decision came into his face. He had made up his mind to his course of action, and his frigid lips and cheeks crackled into a chuckle over it. The pails were already skinned over with young ice when he picked them up and made for the cabin.

When he entered he found the other man waiting, standing near the stove, a certain stiff awkwardness and indecision in his manner. Messner set down his water-pails.

"Glad to meet you, Graham Womble," he said in conventional tones, as though acknowledging an introduction.

Messner did not offer his hand. Womble stirred uneasily, feeling for the other the hatred one is prone to feel for one he has wronged.

"And so you're the chap," Messner said in marvelling accents. "Well, well. You see, I really am glad to meet you. I have been—er—curious to know what Theresa found in you—where, I may say, the attraction lay. Well, well."

And he looked the other up and down as a man would look a horse up and down.

"I know how you must feel about me," Womble began.

"Don't mention it," Messner broke in with exaggerated cordiality of voice and manner. "Never mind that. What I want to know is how do you find her? Up to expectations? Has she worn well? Life been all a happy dream ever since?"

"Don't be silly," Theresa interjected.

"I can't help being natural," Messner complained.

"You can be expedient at the same time, and practical," Womble said sharply. "What we want to know is what are you going to do?"

Messner made a well-feigned gesture of helplessness. "I really don't know. It is one of those impossible situations against which there can be no provision."

"All three of us cannot remain the night in this cabin."

Messner nodded affirmation.

"Then somebody must get out."

"That also is incontrovertible," Messner agreed. "When three bodies cannot occupy the same space at the same time, one must get out."

"And you're that one," Womble announced grimly. "It's a ten-mile pull to the next camp, but you can make it all right."

"And that's the first flaw in your reasoning," the other objected. "Why, necessarily, should I be the one to get out? I found this cabin first."

"But Tess can't get out," Womble explained. "Her lungs are already slightly chilled."

"I agree with you. She can't venture ten miles of frost. By all means she must remain."

"Then it is as I said," Womble announced with finality.

Messner cleared his throat. "Your lungs are all right, aren't they?"

"Yes, but what of it?"

Again the other cleared his throat and spoke with painstaking and judicial slowness. "Why, I may say, nothing of it, except, ah, according to your own reasoning, there is nothing to prevent your getting out, hitting the frost, so to speak, for a matter of ten miles. You can make it all right."

Womble looked with quick suspicion at Theresa and caught in her eyes a glint of pleased surprise.

"Well?" he demanded of her.

She hesitated, and a surge of anger darkened his face. He turned upon Messner.

"Enough of this. You can't stop here."

"Yes, I can."

"I won't let you." Womble squared his shoulders. "I'm running things."

"I'll stay anyway," the other persisted.

"I'll put you out."

"I'll come back."

JACK LONDON

Womble stopped a moment to steady his voice and control himself. Then he spoke slowly, in a low, tense voice.

"Look here, Messner, if you refuse to get out, I'll thrash you. This isn't California. I'll beat you to a jelly with my two fists."

Messner shrugged his shoulders. "If you do, I'll call a miners' meeting and see you strung up to the nearest tree. As you said, this is not California. They're a simple folk, these miners, and all I'll have to do will be to show them the marks of the beating, tell them the truth about you, and present my claim for my wife."

The woman attempted to speak, but Womble turned upon her fiercely.

"You keep out of this," he cried.

In marked contrast was Messner's "Please don't intrude, Theresa."

What of her anger and pent feelings, her lungs were irritated into the dry, hacking cough, and with blood-suffused face and one hand clenched against her chest, she waited for the paroxysm to pass.

Womble looked gloomily at her, noting her cough.

"Something must be done," he said. "Yet her lungs can't stand the exposure. She can't travel till the temperature rises. And I'm not going to give her up."

Messner hemmed, cleared his throat, and hemmed again, semi-apologetically, and said, "I need some money."

Contempt showed instantly in Womble's face. At last, beneath him in vileness, had the other sunk himself.

"You've got a fat sack of dust," Messner went on. "I saw you unload it from the sled."

"How much do you want?" Womble demanded, with a contempt in his voice equal to that in his face.

"I made an estimate of the sack, and I—ah—should say it weighed about twenty pounds. What do you say we call it four thousand?"

"But it's all I've got, man!" Womble cried out.

"You've got her," the other said soothingly. "She must be worth it. Think what I'm giving up. Surely it is a reasonable price."

"All right." Womble rushed across the floor to the gold-sack. "Can't put this deal through too quick for me, you—you little worm!"

"Now, there you err," was the smiling rejoinder. "As a matter of ethics isn't the man who gives a bribe as bad as the man who takes a bribe? The receiver is as bad as the thief, you know; and you needn't console yourself with any fictitious moral superiority concerning this little deal."

"To hell with your ethics!" the other burst out. "Come here and watch the weighing of this dust. I might cheat you."

And the woman, leaning against the bunk, raging and impotent, watched herself weighed out in yellow dust and nuggets in the scales erected on the grub-box. The scales were small, making necessary many weighings, and Messner with precise care verified each weighing.

"There's too much silver in it," he remarked as he tied up the gold-sack. "I don't think it will run quite sixteen to the ounce. You got a trifle the better of me, Womble."

He handled the sack lovingly, and with due appreciation of its preciousness carried it out to his sled.

Returning, he gathered his pots and pans together, packed his grub-box, and rolled up his bed. When the sled was lashed and the complaining dogs harnessed, he returned into the cabin for his mittens.

"Good-by, Tess," he said, standing at the open door.

She turned on him, struggling for speech but too frantic to word the passion that burned in her.

"Good-by, Tess," he repeated gently.

"Beast!" she managed to articulate.

She turned and tottered to the bunk, flinging herself face down upon it, sobbing: "You beasts! You beasts!"

John Messner closed the door softly behind him, and, as he started the dogs, looked back at the cabin with a great relief in his face. At the bottom of the bank, beside the water-hole, he halted the sled. He worked the sack of gold out between the lashings and carried it to the water-hole. Already a new skin of ice had formed. This he broke with his fist. Untying the knotted mouth with his teeth, he emptied the contents of the sack into the water. The river was shallow at that point, and two feet beneath the surface he could see the bottom dull-yellow in the fading light. At the sight of it, he spat into the hole.

He started the dogs along the Yukon trail. Whining spiritlessly, they were reluctant to work. Clinging to the gee-pole with his right band and with his left rubbing cheeks and nose, he stumbled over the rope as the dogs swung on a bend.

"Mush-on, you poor, sore-footed brutes!" he cried. "That's it, mush-on!"

# The White Man's Way

T o cook by your fire and to sleep under your roof for the night," I
had announced on entering old Ebbits's cabin; and he had looked
at me blear-eyed and vacuous, while Zilla had favored me with a sour
face and a contemptuous grunt. Zilla was his wife, and no more bitter-
tongued, implacable old squaw dwelt on the Yukon. Nor would I have
stopped there had my dogs been less tired or had the rest of the village
been inhabited. But this cabin alone had I found occupied, and in this
cabin, perforce, I took my shelter.

Old Ebbits now and again pulled his tangled wits together, and
hints and sparkles of intelligence came and went in his eyes. Several
times during the preparation of my supper he even essayed hospitable
inquiries about my health, the condition and number of my dogs, and
the distance I had travelled that day. And each time Zilla had looked
sourer than ever and grunted more contemptuously.

Yet I confess that there was no particular call for cheerfulness on
their part. There they crouched by the fire, the pair of them, at the end
of their days, old and withered and helpless, racked by rheumatism,
bitten by hunger, and tantalized by the frying-odors of my abundance
of meat. They rocked back and forth in a slow and hopeless way, and
regularly, once every five minutes, Ebbits emitted a low groan. It was
not so much a groan of pain, as of pain-weariness. He was oppressed by
the weight and the torment of this thing called life, and still more was
he oppressed by the fear of death. His was that eternal tragedy of the
aged, with whom the joy of life has departed and the instinct for death
has not come.

When my moose-meat spluttered rowdily in the frying-pan, I
noticed old Ebbits's nostrils twitch and distend as he caught the food-
scent. He ceased rocking for a space and forgot to groan, while a look
of intelligence seemed to come into his face.

Zilla, on the other hand, rocked more rapidly, and for the first
time, in sharp little yelps, voiced her pain. It came to me that their
behavior was like that of hungry dogs, and in the fitness of things I
should not have been astonished had Zilla suddenly developed a tail
and thumped it on the floor in right doggish fashion. Ebbits drooled a
little and stopped his rocking very frequently to lean forward and thrust
his tremulous nose nearer to the source of gustatory excitement.

When I passed them each a plate of the fried meat, they ate greedily, making loud mouth-noises—champings of worn teeth and sucking intakes of the breath, accompanied by a continuous spluttering and mumbling. After that, when I gave them each a mug of scalding tea, the noises ceased. Easement and content came into their faces. Zilla relaxed her sour mouth long enough to sigh her satisfaction. Neither rocked any more, and they seemed to have fallen into placid meditation. Then a dampness came into Ebbits's eyes, and I knew that the sorrow of self-pity was his. The search required to find their pipes told plainly that they had been without tobacco a long time, and the old man's eagerness for the narcotic rendered him helpless, so that I was compelled to light his pipe for him.

"Why are you all alone in the village?" I asked. "Is everybody dead? Has there been a great sickness? Are you alone left of the living?"

Old Ebbits shook his head, saying: "Nay, there has been no great sickness. The village has gone away to hunt meat. We be too old, our legs are not strong, nor can our backs carry the burdens of camp and trail. Wherefore we remain here and wonder when the young men will return with meat."

"What if the young men do return with meat?" Zilla demanded harshly.

"They may return with much meat," he quavered hopefully.

"Even so, with much meat," she continued, more harshly than before. "But of what worth to you and me? A few bones to gnaw in our toothless old age. But the back-fat, the kidneys, and the tongues—these shall go into other mouths than thine and mine, old man."

Ebbits nodded his head and wept silently.

"There be no one to hunt meat for us," she cried, turning fiercely upon me.

There was accusation in her manner, and I shrugged my shoulders in token that I was not guilty of the unknown crime imputed to me.

"Know, O White Man, that it is because of thy kind, because of all white men, that my man and I have no meat in our old age and sit without tobacco in the cold."

"Nay," Ebbits said gravely, with a stricter sense of justice. "Wrong has been done us, it be true; but the white men did not mean the wrong."

"Where be Moklan?" she demanded. "Where be thy strong son, Moklan, and the fish he was ever willing to bring that you might eat?"

The old man shook his head.

"And where be Bidarshik, thy strong son? Ever was he a mighty hunter, and ever did he bring thee the good back-fat and the sweet dried tongues of the moose and the caribou. I see no back-fat and no sweet dried tongues. Your stomach is full with emptiness through the days, and it is for a man of a very miserable and lying people to give you to eat."

"Nay," old Ebbits interposed in kindliness, "the white man's is not a lying people. The white man speaks true. Always does the white man speak true." He paused, casting about him for words wherewith to temper the severity of what he was about to say. "But the white man speaks true in different ways. To-day he speaks true one way, to-morrow he speaks true another way, and there is no understanding him nor his way."

"To-day speak true one way, to-morrow speak true another way, which is to lie," was Zilla's dictum.

"There is no understanding the white man," Ebbits went on doggedly. The meat, and the tea, and the tobacco seemed to have brought him back to life, and he gripped tighter hold of the idea behind his age-bleared eyes. He straightened up somewhat. His voice lost its querulous and whimpering note, and became strong and positive. He turned upon me with dignity, and addressed me as equal addresses equal.

"The white man's eyes are not shut," he began. "The white man sees all things, and thinks greatly, and is very wise. But the white man of one day is not the white man of next day, and there is no understanding him. He does not do things always in the same way. And what way his next way is to be, one cannot know. Always does the Indian do the one thing in the one way. Always does the moose come down from the high mountains when the winter is here. Always does the salmon come in the spring when the ice has gone out of the river. Always does everything do all things in the same way, and the Indian knows and understands. But the white man does not do all things in the same way, and the Indian does not know nor understand.

"Tobacco be very good. It be food to the hungry man. It makes the strong man stronger, and the angry man to forget that he is angry. Also is tobacco of value. It is of very great value. The Indian gives one large salmon for one leaf of tobacco, and he chews the tobacco for a long time. It is the juice of the tobacco that is good. When it runs down his throat it makes him feel good inside. But the white man! When his mouth is full with the juice, what does he do? That juice, that juice of great value, he spits it out in the snow and it is lost. Does the white man like tobacco? I do not know. But if he likes tobacco, why does he spit out its value and lose it in the snow? It is a great foolishness and without understanding."

He ceased, puffed at the pipe, found that it was out, and passed it over to Zilla, who took the sneer at the white man off her lips in order to pucker them about the pipe-stem. Ebbits seemed sinking back into his senility with the tale untold, and I demanded:

"What of thy sons, Moklan and Bidarshik? And why is it that you and your old woman are without meat at the end of your years?"

He roused himself as from sleep, and straightened up with an effort.

"It is not good to steal," he said. "When the dog takes your meat you beat the dog with a club. Such is the law. It is the law the man gave to the dog, and the dog must live to the law, else will it suffer the pain of the club. When man takes your meat, or your canoe, or your wife, you kill that man. That is the law, and it is a good law. It is not good to steal, wherefore it is the law that the man who steals must die. Whoso breaks the law must suffer hurt. It is a great hurt to die."

"But if you kill the man, why do you not kill the dog?" I asked.

Old Ebbits looked at me in childlike wonder, while Zilla sneered openly at the absurdity of my question.

"It is the way of the white man," Ebbits mumbled with an air of resignation.

"It is the foolishness of the white man," snapped Zilla.

"Then let old Ebbits teach the white man wisdom," I said softly.

"The dog is not killed, because it must pull the sled of the man. No man pulls another man's sled, wherefore the man is killed."

"Oh," I murmured.

"That is the law," old Ebbits went on. "Now listen, O White Man, and I will tell you of a great foolishness. There is an Indian. His name is Mobits. From white man he steals two pounds of flour. What does the white man do? Does he beat Mobits? No. Does he kill Mobits? No. What does he do to Mobits? I will tell you, O White Man. He has a house. He puts Mobits in that house. The roof is good. The walls are thick. He makes a fire that Mobits may be warm. He gives Mobits plenty grub to eat. It is good grub. Never in his all days does Mobits eat so good grub. There is bacon, and bread, and beans without end. Mobits have very good time.

"There is a big lock on door so that Mobits does not run away. This also is a great foolishness. Mobits will not run away. All the time is there plenty grub in that place, and warm blankets, and a big fire. Very foolish to run away. Mobits is not foolish. Three months Mobits stop in that place. He steal two pounds of flour. For that, white man take plenty good care of him. Mobits eat many pounds of flour, many pounds of sugar, of bacon, of beans without end. Also, Mobits drink much tea. After three months white man open door and tell Mobits he must go. Mobits does not want to go. He is like dog that is fed long time in one place. He want to stay in that place, and the white man must drive Mobits away. So Mobits come back to this village, and he is very fat. That is the white man's way, and there is no understanding it. It is a foolishness, a great foolishness."

"But thy sons?" I insisted. "Thy very strong sons and thine old-age hunger?"

"There was Moklan," Ebbits began.

"A strong man," interrupted the mother. "He could dip paddle all of a day and night and never stop for the need of rest. He was wise in the way of the salmon and in the way of the water. He was very wise."

"There was Moklan," Ebbits repeated, ignoring the interruption. "In the spring, he went down the Yukon with the young men to trade at Cambell Fort. There is a post there, filled with the goods of the white man, and a trader whose name is Jones. Likewise is there a white man's medicine man, what you call missionary. Also is there bad water at Cambell Fort, where the Yukon goes slim like a maiden, and the water is fast, and the currents rush this way and that and come together, and there are whirls and sucks, and always are the currents changing and the face of the water changing, so at any two times it is never the same. Moklan is my son, wherefore he is brave man—"

"Was not my father brave man?" Zilla demanded.

"Thy father was brave man," Ebbits acknowledged, with the air of one who will keep peace in the house at any cost. "Moklan is thy son and mine, wherefore he is brave. Mayhap, because of thy very brave father, Moklan is too brave. It is like when too much water is put in the pot it spills over. So too much bravery is put into Moklan, and the bravery spills over.

"The young men are much afraid of the bad water at Cambell Fort. But Moklan is not afraid. He laughs strong, Ho! ho! and he goes forth into the bad water. But where the currents come together the canoe is turned over. A whirl takes Moklan by the legs, and he goes around and around, and down and down, and is seen no more."

"Ai! ai!" wailed Zilla. "Crafty and wise was he, and my first-born!"

"I am the father of Moklan," Ebbits said, having patiently given the woman space for her noise. "I get into canoe and journey down to Cambell Fort to collect the debt!"

"Debt!" interrupted. "What debt?"

"The debt of Jones, who is chief trader," came the answer. "Such is the law of travel in a strange country."

I shook my head in token of my ignorance, and Ebbits looked compassion at me, while Zilla snorted her customary contempt.

"Look you, O White Man," he said. "In thy camp is a dog that bites. When the dog bites a man, you give that man a present because you are sorry and because it is thy dog. You make payment. Is it not so? Also, if you have in thy country bad hunting, or bad water, you must make payment. It is just. It is the law. Did not my father's brother go over into the Tanana Country and get killed by a bear? And did not the Tanana tribe pay my father many blankets and fine furs? It was just. It was bad hunting, and the Tanana people made payment for the bad hunting.

"So I, Ebbits, journeyed down to Cambell Fort to collect the debt. Jones, who is chief trader, looked at me, and he laughed. He made great laughter, and would not give payment. I went to the medicine-man, what you call missionary, and had large talk about the bad water and the payment that should be mine. And the missionary made talk about other things. He talk about where Moklan has gone, now he is dead. There be large fires in that place, and if missionary make true talk, I know that Moklan will be cold no more. Also the missionary talk about where I shall go when I am dead. And he say bad things. He say that I am blind. Which is a lie. He say that I am in great darkness. Which is a lie. And I say that the day come and the night come for everybody just the same, and that in my village it is no more dark than at Cambell Fort. Also, I say that darkness and light and where we go when we die be different things from the matter of payment of just debt for bad water. Then the missionary make large anger, and call me bad names of darkness, and tell me to go away. And so I come back from Cambell Fort, and no payment has been made, and Moklan is dead, and in my old age I am without fish and meat."

"Because of the white man," said Zilla.

"Because of the white man," Ebbits concurred. "And other things because of the white man. There was Bidarshik. One way did the white man deal with him; and yet another way for the same thing did the white man deal with Yamikan. And first must I tell you of Yamikan, who was a young man of this village and who chanced to kill a white man. It is not good to kill a man of another people. Always is there great trouble. It was not the fault of Yamikan that he killed the white man. Yamikan spoke always soft words and ran away from wrath as a dog from a stick. But this white man drank much whiskey, and in the night-time came to Yamikan's house and made much fight. Yamikan cannot run away, and the white man tries to kill him. Yamikan does not like to die, so he kills the white man.

"Then is all the village in great trouble. We are much afraid that we must make large payment to the white man's people, and we hide our blankets, and our furs, and all our wealth, so that it will seem that we are poor people and can make only small payment. After long time white men come. They are soldier white men, and they take Yamikan away with them. His mother make great noise and throw ashes in her hair, for she knows Yamikan is dead. And all the village knows that Yamikan is dead, and is glad that no payment is asked.

"That is in the spring when the ice has gone out of the river. One year go by, two years go by. It is spring-time again, and the ice has gone out of the river. And then Yamikan, who is dead, comes back to us, and he is not dead, but very fat, and we know that he has slept warm and had plenty grub to eat. He has much fine clothes and is all the same white man, and he has gathered large wisdom so that he is very quick head man in the village.

"And he has strange things to tell of the way of the white man, for he has seen much of the white man and done a great travel into the white man's country. First place, soldier white men take him down the river long way. All the way do they take him down the river to the end, where it runs into a lake which is larger than all the land and large as the sky. I do not know the Yukon is so big river, but Yamikan has seen with his own eyes. I do not think there is a lake larger than all the land and large as the sky, but Yamikan has seen. Also, he has told me that the waters of this lake be salt, which is a strange thing and beyond understanding.

"But the White Man knows all these marvels for himself, so I shall not weary him with the telling of them. Only will I tell him what happened to Yamikan. The white man give Yamikan much fine grub. All the time does Yamikan eat, and all the time is there plenty more grub. The white man lives under the sun, so said Yamikan, where there be much warmth, and animals have only hair and no fur, and the green things grow large and strong and become flour, and beans, and potatoes. And under the sun there is never famine. Always is there plenty grub. I do not know. Yamikan has said.

"And here is a strange thing that befell Yamikan. Never did the white man hurt him. Only did they give him warm bed at night and plenty fine grub. They take him across the salt lake which is big as the sky. He is on white man's fire-boat, what you call steamboat, only he is on boat maybe twenty times bigger than steamboat on Yukon. Also, it is made of iron, this boat, and yet does it not sink. This I do not understand, but Yamikan has said, 'I have journeyed far on the iron boat; behold! I am still alive.' It is a white man's soldier-boat with many soldier men upon it.

"After many sleeps of travel, a long, long time, Yamikan comes to a land where there is no snow. I cannot believe this. It is not in the nature of things that when winter comes there shall be no snow. But Yamikan has seen. Also have I asked the white men, and they have said yes, there is no snow in that country. But I cannot believe, and now I ask you if snow never come in that country. Also, I would hear the name of that country. I have heard the name before, but I would hear it again, if it be the same—thus will I know if I have heard lies or true talk."

Old Ebbits regarded me with a wistful face. He would have the truth at any cost, though it was his desire to retain his faith in the marvel he had never seen.

"Yes," I answered, "it is true talk that you have heard. There is no snow in that country, and its name is California."

"Cal-ee-forn-ee-yeh," he mumbled twice and thrice, listening intently to the sound of the syllables as they fell from his lips. He nodded his head in confirmation. "Yes, it is the same country of which Yamikan made talk."

I recognized the adventure of Yamikan as one likely to occur in the early days when Alaska first passed into the possession of the United States. Such a murder case, occurring before the instalment of territorial law and officials, might well have been taken down to the United States for trial before a Federal court.

"When Yamikan is in this country where there is no snow," old Ebbits continued, "he is taken to large house where many men make much talk. Long time men talk. Also many questions do they ask Yamikan. By and by they tell Yamikan he have no more trouble. Yamikan does not understand, for never has he had any trouble. All the time have they given him warm place to sleep and plenty grub.

"But after that they give him much better grub, and they give him money, and they take him many places in white man's country, and he see many strange things which are beyond the understanding of Ebbits, who is an old man and has not journeyed far. After two years, Yamikan comes back to this village, and he is head man, and very wise until he dies.

"But before he dies, many times does he sit by my fire and make talk of the strange things he has seen. And Bidarshik, who is my son, sits by the fire and listens; and his eyes are very wide and large because of the things he hears. One night, after Yamikan has gone home, Bidarshik stands up, so, very tall, and he strikes his chest with his fist, and says, 'When I am a man, I shall journey in far places, even to the land where there is no snow, and see things for myself.'"

"Always did Bidarshik journey in far places," Zilla interrupted proudly.

"It be true," Ebbits assented gravely. "And always did he return to sit by the fire and hunger for yet other and unknown far places."

"And always did he remember the salt lake as big as the sky and the country under the sun where there is no snow," quoth Zilla.

"And always did he say, 'When I have the full strength of a man, I will go and see for myself if the talk of Yamikan be true talk,'" said Ebbits.

"But there was no way to go to the white man's country," said Zilla.

"Did he not go down to the salt lake that is big as the sky?" Ebbits demanded.

"And there was no way for him across the salt lake," said Zilla.

"Save in the white man's fire-boat which is of iron and is bigger than twenty steamboats on the Yukon," said Ebbits. He scowled at Zilla, whose withered lips were again writhing into speech, and compelled her to silence. "But the white man would not let him cross the salt lake in the fire-boat, and he returned to sit by the fire and hunger for the country under the sun where there is no snow.'"

"Yet on the salt lake had he seen the fire-boat of iron that did not sink," cried out Zilla the irrepressible.

"Ay," said Ebbits, "and he saw that Yamikan had made true talk of the things he had seen. But there was no way for Bidarshik to journey to the white man's land under the sun, and he grew sick and weary like an old man and moved not away from the fire. No longer did he go forth to kill meat—"

"And no longer did he eat the meat placed before him," Zilla broke in. "He would shake his head and say, 'Only do I care to eat the grub of the white man and grow fat after the manner of Yamikan.'"

"And he did not eat the meat," Ebbits went on. "And the sickness of Bidarshik grew into a great sickness until I thought he would die. It was not a sickness of the body, but of the head. It was a sickness of desire. I, Ebbits, who am his father, make a great think. I have no more sons and I do not want Bidarshik to die. It is a head-sickness, and there is but one way to make it well. Bidarshik must journey across the lake as large as the sky to the land where there is no snow, else will he die. I make a very great think, and then I see the way for Bidarshik to go.

"So, one night when he sits by the fire, very sick, his head hanging down, I say, 'My son, I have learned the way for you to go to the white man's land.' He looks at me, and his face is glad. 'Go,' I say, 'even as Yamikan went.' But Bidarshik is sick and does not understand. 'Go forth,' I say, 'and find a white man, and, even as Yamikan, do you kill that white man. Then will the soldier white men come and get you, and even as they took Yamikan will they take you across the salt lake to the white man's land. And then, even as Yamikan, will you return very fat, your eyes full of the things you have seen, your head filled with wisdom.'

"And Bidarshik stands up very quick, and his hand is reaching out for his gun. 'Where do you go?' I ask. 'To kill the white man,' he says. And I see that my words have been good in the ears of Bidarshik and that he will grow well again. Also do I know that my words have been wise.

"There is a white man come to this village. He does not seek after gold in the ground, nor after furs in the forest. All the time does he seek after bugs and flies. He does not eat the bugs and flies, then why does he seek after them? I do not know. Only do I know that he is a funny white man. Also does he seek after the eggs of birds. He does not eat the eggs. All that is inside he takes out, and only does he keep the shell. Eggshell is not good to eat. Nor does he eat the eggshells, but puts them away in soft boxes where they will not break. He catch many small birds. But he does not eat the birds. He takes only the skins and puts them away in boxes. Also does he like bones. Bones are not good to eat. And this strange white man likes best the bones of long time ago which he digs out of the ground.

"But he is not a fierce white man, and I know he will die very easy; so I say to Bidarshik, 'My son, there is the white man for you to kill.' And Bidarshik says that my words be wise. So he goes to a place he knows where are many bones in the ground. He digs up very many of these bones and brings them to the strange white man's camp. The white man is made very glad. His face shines like the sun, and he smiles with much gladness as he looks at the bones. He bends his head over, so, to look well at the bones, and then Bidarshik strikes him hard on the head, with axe, once, so, and the strange white man kicks and is dead.

"'Now,' I say to Bidarshik, 'will the white soldier men come and take you away to the land under the sun, where you will eat much and grow fat.' Bidarshik is happy. Already has his sickness gone from him, and he sits by the fire and waits for the coming of the white soldier men.

"How was I to know the way of the white man is never twice the same?" the old man demanded, whirling upon me fiercely. "How was I to know that what the white man does yesterday he will not do to-day, and that what he does to-day he will not do to-morrow?" Ebbits shook his head sadly. "There is no understanding the white man. Yesterday he takes Yamikan to the land under the sun and makes him fat with much grub. To-day he takes Bidarshik and—what does he do with Bidarshik? Let me tell you what he does with Bidarshik.

"I, Ebbits, his father, will tell you. He takes Bidarshik to Cambell Fort, and he ties a rope around his neck, so, and, when his feet are no more on the ground, he dies."

"Ai! ai!" wailed Zilla. "And never does he cross the lake large as the sky, nor see the land under the sun where there is no snow."

"Wherefore," old Ebbits said with grave dignity, "there be no one to hunt meat for me in my old age, and I sit hungry by my fire and tell my story to the White Man who has given me grub, and strong tea, and tobacco for my pipe."

"Because of the lying and very miserable white people," Zilla proclaimed shrilly.

"Nay," answered the old man with gentle positiveness. "Because of the way of the white man, which is without understanding and never twice the same."

# The Story of Keesh

K eesh lived long ago on the rim of the polar sea, was head man of his village through many and prosperous years, and died full of honors with his name on the lips of men. So long ago did he live that only the old men remember his name, his name and the tale, which they got from the old men before them, and which the old men to come will tell to their children and their children's children down to the end of time. And the winter darkness, when the north gales make their long sweep across the ice-pack, and the air is filled with flying white, and no man may venture forth, is the chosen time for the telling of how Keesh, from the poorest *igloo* in the village, rose to power and place over them all.

He was a bright boy, so the tale runs, healthy and strong, and he had seen thirteen suns, in their way of reckoning time. For each winter the sun leaves the land in darkness, and the next year a new sun returns so that they may be warm again and look upon one another's faces. The father of Keesh had been a very brave man, but he had met his death in a time of famine, when he sought to save the lives of his people by taking the life of a great polar bear. In his eagerness he came to close grapples with the bear, and his bones were crushed; but the bear had much meat on him and the people were saved. Keesh was his only son, and after that Keesh lived alone with his mother. But the people are prone to forget, and they forgot the deed of his father; and he being but a boy, and his mother only a woman, they, too, were swiftly forgotten, and ere long came to live in the meanest of all the *igloos*.

It was at a council, one night, in the big *igloo* of Klosh-Kwan, the chief, that Keesh showed the blood that ran in his veins and the manhood that stiffened his back. With the dignity of an elder, he rose to his feet, and waited for silence amid the babble of voices.

"It is true that meat be apportioned me and mine," he said. "But it is ofttimes old and tough, this meat, and, moreover, it has an unusual quantity of bones."

The hunters, grizzled and gray, and lusty and young, were aghast. The like had never been known before. A child, that talked like a grown man, and said harsh things to their very faces!

But steadily and with seriousness, Keesh went on. "For that I know my father, Bok, was a great hunter, I speak these words. It is said that Bok brought home more meat than any of the two best hunters, that with his own hands he attended to the division of it, that with his own eyes he saw to it that the least old woman and the last old man received fair share."

"Na! Na!" the men cried. "Put the child out!" "Send him off to bed!" "He is no man that he should talk to men and graybeards!"

He waited calmly till the uproar died down.

"Thou hast a wife, Ugh-Gluk," he said, "and for her dost thou speak. And thou, too, Massuk, a mother also, and for them dost thou speak. My mother has no one, save me; wherefore I speak. As I say, though Bok be dead because he hunted over-keenly, it is just that I, who am his son, and that Ikeega, who is my mother and was his wife, should have meat in plenty so long as there be meat in plenty in the tribe. I, Keesh, the son of Bok, have spoken."

He sat down, his ears keenly alert to the flood of protest and indignation his words had created.

"That a boy should speak in council!" old Ugh-Gluk was mumbling.

"Shall the babes in arms tell us men the things we shall do?" Massuk demanded in a loud voice. "Am I a man that I should be made a mock by every child that cries for meat?"

The anger boiled a white heat. They ordered him to bed, threatened that he should have no meat at all, and promised him sore beatings for his presumption. Keesh's eyes began to flash, and the blood to pound darkly under his skin. In the midst of the abuse he sprang to his feet.

"Hear me, ye men!" he cried. "Never shall I speak in the council again, never again till the men come to me and say, 'It is well, Keesh, that thou shouldst speak, it is well and it is our wish.' Take this now, ye men, for my last word. Bok, my father, was a great hunter. I, too, his son, shall go and hunt the meat that I eat. And be it known, now, that the division of that which I kill shall be fair. And no widow nor weak one shall cry in the night because there is no meat, when the strong men are groaning in great pain for that they have eaten overmuch. And in the days to come there shall be shame upon the strong men who have eaten overmuch. I, Keesh, have said it!"

Jeers and scornful laughter followed him out of the *igloo*, but his jaw was set and he went his way, looking neither to right nor left.

The next day he went forth along the shore-line where the ice and the land met together. Those who saw him go noted that he carried his bow, with a goodly supply of bone-barbed arrows, and that across his shoulder was his father's big hunting-spear. And there was laughter, and much talk, at the event. It was an unprecedented occurrence. Never did boys of his tender age go forth to hunt, much less to hunt alone. Also were there shaking of heads and prophetic mutterings, and the women looked pityingly at Ikeega, and her face was grave and sad.

"He will be back ere long," they said cheeringly.

"Let him go; it will teach him a lesson," the hunters said. "And he will come back shortly, and he will be meek and soft of speech in the days to follow."

But a day passed, and a second, and on the third a wild gale blew, and there was no Keesh. Ikeega tore her hair and put soot of the seal-oil on her face in token of her grief; and the women assailed the men with bitter words in that they had mistreated the boy and sent him to his death; and the men made no answer, preparing to go in search of the body when the storm abated.

Early next morning, however, Keesh strode into the village. But he came not shamefacedly. Across his shoulders he bore a burden of fresh-killed meat. And there was importance in his step and arrogance in his speech.

"Go, ye men, with the dogs and sledges, and take my trail for the better part of a day's travel," he said. "There is much meat on the ice—a she-bear and two half-grown cubs."

Ikeega was overcome with joy, but he received her demonstrations in manlike fashion, saying: "Come, Ikeega, let us eat. And after that I shall sleep, for I am weary."

And he passed into their *igloo* and ate profoundly, and after that slept for twenty running hours.

There was much doubt at first, much doubt and discussion. The killing of a polar bear is very dangerous, but thrice dangerous is it, and three times thrice, to kill a mother bear with her cubs. The men could not bring themselves to believe that the boy Keesh, single-handed, had accomplished so great a marvel. But the women spoke of the fresh-killed meat he had brought on his back, and this was an overwhelming argument against their unbelief. So they finally departed, grumbling greatly that in all probability, if the thing were so, he had neglected to cut up the carcasses. Now in the north it is very necessary that this should be done as soon as a kill is made. If not, the meat freezes so solidly as to turn the edge of the sharpest knife, and a three-hundred-pound bear, frozen stiff, is no easy thing to put upon a sled and haul over the rough ice. But arrived at the spot, they found not only the kill, which they had doubted, but that Keesh had quartered the beasts in true hunter fashion, and removed the entrails.

Thus began the mystery of Keesh, a mystery that deepened and deepened with the passing of the days. His very next trip he killed a young bear, nearly full-grown, and on the trip following, a large male bear and his mate. He was ordinarily gone from three to four days, though it was nothing unusual for him to stay away a week at a time on the ice-field. Always he declined company on these expeditions, and the people marvelled. "How does he do it?" they demanded of one another. "Never does he take a dog with him, and dogs are of such great help, too."

"Why dost thou hunt only bear?" Klosh-Kwan once ventured to ask him.

And Keesh made fitting answer. "It is well known that there is more meat on the bear," he said.

But there was also talk of witchcraft in the village. "He hunts with evil spirits," some of the people contended, "wherefore his hunting is rewarded. How else can it be, save that he hunts with evil spirits?"

"Mayhap they be not evil, but good, these spirits," others said. "It is known that his father was a mighty hunter. May not his father hunt with him so that he may attain excellence and patience and understanding? Who knows?"

None the less, his success continued, and the less skilful hunters were often kept busy hauling in his meat. And in the division of it he was just. As his father had done before him, he saw to it that the least old woman and the last old man received a fair portion, keeping no more for himself than his needs required. And because of this, and of his merit as a hunter, he was looked upon with respect, and even awe; and there was talk of making him chief after old Klosh-Kwan. Because of the things he had done, they looked for him to appear again in the council, but he never came, and they were ashamed to ask.

"I am minded to build me an *igloo*," he said one day to Klosh-Kwan and a number of the hunters. "It shall be a large *igloo*, wherein Ikeega and I can dwell in comfort."

"Ay," they nodded gravely.

"But I have no time. My business is hunting, and it takes all my time. So it is but just that the men and women of the village who eat my meat should build me my *igloo*."

And the *igloo* was built accordingly, on a generous scale which exceeded even the dwelling of Klosh-Kwan. Keesh and his mother moved into it, and it was the first prosperity she had enjoyed since the death of Bok. Nor was material prosperity alone hers, for, because of her wonderful son and the position he had given her, she came to be looked upon as the first woman in all the village; and the women were given to visiting her, to asking her advice, and to quoting her wisdom when arguments arose among themselves or with the men.

But it was the mystery of Keesh's marvellous hunting that took chief place in all their minds. And one day Ugh-Gluk taxed him with witchcraft to his face.

"It is charged," Ugh-Gluk said ominously, "that thou dealest with evil spirits, wherefore thy hunting is rewarded."

"Is not the meat good?" Keesh made answer. "Has one in the village yet to fall sick from the eating of it? How dost thou know that witchcraft be concerned? Or dost thou guess, in the dark, merely because of the envy that consumes thee?"

And Ugh-Gluk withdrew discomfited, the women laughing at him as he walked away. But in the council one night, after long deliberation, it was determined to put spies on his track when he went forth to hunt, so that his methods might be learned. So, on his next trip, Bim and Bawn, two young men, and of hunters the craftiest, followed after him, taking care not to be seen. After five days they returned, their eyes bulging and their tongues a-tremble to tell what they had seen. The council was hastily called in Klosh-Kwan's dwelling, and Bim took up the tale.

"Brothers! As commanded, we journeyed on the trail of Keesh, and cunningly we journeyed, so that he might not know. And midway of the first day he picked up with a great he-bear. It was a very great bear."

"None greater," Bawn corroborated, and went on himself. "Yet was the bear not inclined to fight, for he turned away and made off slowly over the ice. This we saw from the rocks of the shore, and the bear came toward us, and after him came Keesh, very much unafraid. And he shouted harsh words after the bear, and waved his arms about, and made much noise. Then did the bear grow angry, and rise up on his hind legs, and growl. But Keesh walked right up to the bear."

"Ay," Bim continued the story. "Right up to the bear Keesh walked. And the bear took after him, and Keesh ran away. But as he ran he dropped a little round ball on the ice. And the bear stopped and smelled of it, then swallowed it up. And Keesh continued to run away and drop little round balls, and the bear continued to swallow them up."

Exclamations and cries of doubt were being made, and Ugh-Gluk expressed open unbelief.

"With our own eyes we saw it," Bim affirmed.

And Bawn—"Ay, with our own eyes. And this continued until the bear stood suddenly upright and cried aloud in pain, and thrashed his fore paws madly about. And Keesh continued to make off over the ice to a safe distance. But the bear gave him no notice, being occupied with the misfortune the little round balls had wrought within him."

"Ay, within him," Bim interrupted. "For he did claw at himself, and leap about over the ice like a playful puppy, save from the way he growled and squealed it was plain it was not play but pain. Never did I see such a sight!"

"Nay, never was such a sight seen," Bawn took up the strain. "And furthermore, it was such a large bear."

"Witchcraft," Ugh-Gluk suggested.

"I know not," Bawn replied. "I tell only of what my eyes beheld. And after a while the bear grew weak and tired, for he was very heavy and he had jumped about with exceeding violence, and he went off along the shore-ice, shaking his head slowly from side to side and sitting down ever and again to squeal and cry. And Keesh followed after the bear, and we followed after Keesh, and for that day and three days more we followed. The bear grew weak, and never ceased crying from his pain."

"It was a charm!" Ugh-Gluk exclaimed. "Surely it was a charm!"

"It may well be."

And Bim relieved Bawn. "The bear wandered, now this way and now that, doubling back and forth and crossing his trail in circles, so that at the end he was near where Keesh had first come upon him. By this time he was quite sick, the bear, and could crawl no farther, so Keesh came up close and speared him to death."

"And then?" Klosh-Kwan demanded.

"Then we left Keesh skinning the bear, and came running that the news of the killing might be told."

And in the afternoon of that day the women hauled in the meat of the bear while the men sat in council assembled. When Keesh arrived a messenger was sent to him, bidding him come to the council. But he sent reply, saying that he was hungry and tired; also that his *igloo* was large and comfortable and could hold many men.

And curiosity was so strong on the men that the whole council, Klosh-Kwan to the fore, rose up and went to the *igloo* of Keesh. He was eating, but he received them with respect and seated them according to their rank. Ikeega was proud and embarrassed by turns, but Keesh was quite composed.

Klosh-Kwan recited the information brought by Bim and Bawn, and at its close said in a stern voice: "So explanation is wanted, O Keesh, of thy manner of hunting. Is there witchcraft in it?"

Keesh looked up and smiled. "Nay, O Klosh-Kwan. It is not for a boy to know aught of witches, and of witches I know nothing. I have but devised a means whereby I may kill the ice-bear with ease, that is all. It be headcraft, not witchcraft."

"And may any man?"

"Any man."

There was a long silence. The men looked in one another's faces, and Keesh went on eating.

"And. . . and. . . and wilt thou tell us, O Keesh?" Klosh-Kwan finally asked in a tremulous voice.

"Yea, I will tell thee." Keesh finished sucking a marrow-bone and rose to his feet. "It is quite simple. Behold!"

He picked up a thin strip of whalebone and showed it to them. The ends were sharp as needle-points. The strip he coiled carefully, till it disappeared in his hand. Then, suddenly releasing it, it sprang straight again. He picked up a piece of blubber.

"So," he said, "one takes a small chunk of blubber, thus, and thus makes it hollow. Then into the hollow goes the whalebone, so, tightly coiled, and another piece of blubber is fitted over the whale-bone. After that it is put outside where it freezes into a little round ball. The bear swallows the little round ball, the blubber melts, the whalebone with its sharp ends stands out straight, the bear gets sick, and when the bear is very sick, why, you kill him with a spear. It is quite simple."

And Ugh-Gluk said "Oh!" and Klosh-Kwan said "Ah!" And each said something after his own manner, and all understood.

And this is the story of Keesh, who lived long ago on the rim of the polar sea. Because he exercised headcraft and not witchcraft, he rose from the meanest *igloo* to be head man of his village, and through all the years that he lived, it is related, his tribe was prosperous, and neither widow nor weak one cried aloud in the night because there was no meat.

# The Unexpected

It is a simple matter to see the obvious, to do the expected. The tendency of the individual life is to be static rather than dynamic, and this tendency is made into a propulsion by civilization, where the obvious only is seen, and the unexpected rarely happens. When the unexpected does happen, however, and when it is of sufficiently grave import, the unfit perish. They do not see what is not obvious, are unable to do the unexpected, are incapable of adjusting their well-grooved lives to other and strange grooves. In short, when they come to the end of their own groove, they die.

On the other hand, there are those that make toward survival, the fit individuals who escape from the rule of the obvious and the expected and adjust their lives to no matter what strange grooves they may stray into, or into which they may be forced. Such an individual was Edith Whittlesey. She was born in a rural district of England, where life proceeds by rule of thumb and the unexpected is so very unexpected that when it happens it is looked upon as an immorality. She went into service early, and while yet a young woman, by rule-of-thumb progression, she became a lady's maid.

The effect of civilization is to impose human law upon environment until it becomes machine-like in its regularity. The objectionable is eliminated, the inevitable is foreseen. One is not even made wet by the rain nor cold by the frost; while death, instead of stalking about grewsome and accidental, becomes a prearranged pageant, moving along a well-oiled groove to the family vault, where the hinges are kept from rusting and the dust from the air is swept continually away.

Such was the environment of Edith Whittlesey. Nothing happened. It could scarcely be called a happening, when, at the age of twenty-five, she accompanied her mistress on a bit of travel to the United States. The groove merely changed its direction. It was still the same groove and well oiled. It was a groove that bridged the Atlantic with uneventfulness, so that the ship was not a ship in the midst of the sea, but a capacious, many-corridored hotel that moved swiftly and placidly, crushing the waves into submission with its colossal bulk until the sea was a mill-pond, monotonous with quietude. And at the other side the groove continued on over the land—a well-disposed, respectable groove that supplied hotels at every stopping-place, and hotels on wheels between the stopping-places.

In Chicago, while her mistress saw one side of social life, Edith Whittlesey saw another side; and when she left her lady's service and became Edith Nelson, she betrayed, perhaps faintly, her ability to grapple with the unexpected and to master it. Hans Nelson, immigrant, Swede by birth and carpenter by occupation, had in him that Teutonic unrest that drives the race ever westward on its great adventure. He was a large-muscled, stolid sort of a man, in whom little imagination was coupled with immense initiative, and who possessed, withal, loyalty and affection as sturdy as his own strength.

"When I have worked hard and saved me some money, I will go to Colorado," he had told Edith on the day after their wedding. A year later they were in Colorado, where Hans Nelson saw his first mining and caught the mining-fever himself. His prospecting led him through the Dakotas, Idaho, and eastern Oregon, and on into the mountains of British Columbia. In camp and on trail, Edith Nelson was always with him, sharing his luck, his hardship, and his toil. The short step of the house-reared woman she exchanged for the long stride of the mountaineer. She learned to look upon danger clear-eyed and with understanding, losing forever that panic fear which is bred of ignorance and which afflicts the city-reared, making them as silly as silly horses, so that they await fate in frozen horror instead of grappling with it, or stampede in blind self-destroying terror which clutters the way with their crushed carcasses.

Edith Nelson met the unexpected at every turn of the trail, and she trained her vision so that she saw in the landscape, not the obvious, but the concealed. She, who had never cooked in her life, learned to make bread without the mediation of hops, yeast, or baking-powder, and to bake bread, top and bottom, in a frying-pan before an open fire. And when the last cup of flour was gone and the last rind of bacon, she was able to rise to the occasion, and of moccasins and the softer-tanned bits of leather in the outfit to make a grub-stake substitute that somehow held a man's soul in his body and enabled him to stagger on. She learned to pack a horse as well as a man,—a task to break the heart and the pride of any city-dweller, and she knew how to throw the hitch best suited for any particular kind of pack. Also, she could build a fire of wet wood in a downpour of rain and not lose her temper. In short, in all its guises she mastered the unexpected. But the Great Unexpected was yet to come into her life and put its test upon her.

The gold-seeking tide was flooding northward into Alaska, and it was inevitable that Hans Nelson and his wife should he caught up by the stream and swept toward the Klondike. The fall of 1897 found them at Dyea, but without the money to carry an outfit across Chilcoot Pass and float it down to Dawson. So Hans Nelson worked at his trade that winter and helped rear the mushroom outfitting-town of Skaguay.

He was on the edge of things, and throughout the winter he heard all Alaska calling to him. Latuya Bay called loudest, so that the summer of 1898 found him and his wife threading the mazes of the broken coast-line in seventy-foot Siwash canoes. With them were Indians, also three other men. The Indians landed them and their supplies in a lonely bight of land a hundred miles or so beyond Latuya Bay, and returned to Skaguay; but the three other men remained, for they were members of the organized party. Each had put an equal share of capital into the outfitting, and the profits were to be divided equally. In that Edith Nelson undertook to cook for the outfit, a man's share was to be her portion.

First, spruce trees were cut down and a three-room cabin constructed. To keep this cabin was Edith Nelson's task. The task of the men was to search for gold, which they did; and to find gold, which they likewise did. It was not a startling find, merely a low-pay placer where long hours of severe toil earned each man between fifteen and twenty dollars a day. The brief Alaskan summer protracted itself beyond its usual length, and they took advantage of the opportunity, delaying their return to Skaguay to the last moment. And then it was too late. Arrangements had been made to accompany the several dozen local Indians on their fall trading trip down the coast. The Siwashes had waited on the white people until the eleventh hour, and then departed. There was no course left the party but to wait for chance transportation. In the meantime the claim was cleaned up and firewood stocked in.

The Indian summer had dreamed on and on, and then, suddenly, with the sharpness of bugles, winter came. It came in a single night, and the miners awoke to howling wind, driving snow, and freezing water. Storm followed storm, and between the storms there was the silence, broken only by the boom of the surf on the desolate shore, where the salt spray rimmed the beach with frozen white.

All went well in the cabin. Their gold-dust had weighed up something like eight thousand dollars, and they could not but be contented. The men made snowshoes, hunted fresh meat for the larder, and in the long evenings played endless games of whist and pedro. Now that the mining had ceased, Edith Nelson turned over the fire-building and the dish-washing to the men, while she darned their socks and mended their clothes.

There was no grumbling, no bickering, nor petty quarrelling in the little cabin, and they often congratulated one another on the general happiness of the party. Hans Nelson was stolid and easy-going, while Edith had long before won his unbounded admiration by her capacity for getting on with people. Harkey, a long, lank Texan, was unusually friendly for one with a saturnine disposition, and, as long as his theory that gold grew was not challenged, was quite companionable. The fourth member of the party, Michael Dennin, contributed his Irish wit to the gayety of the cabin. He was a large, powerful man, prone to sudden rushes of anger over little things, and of unfailing good-humor under the stress and strain of big things. The fifth and last member, Dutchy, was the willing butt of the party. He even went out of his way to raise a laugh at his own expense in order to keep things cheerful. His deliberate aim in life seemed to be that of a maker of laughter. No serious quarrel had ever vexed the serenity of the party; and, now that each had sixteen hundred dollars to show for a short summer's work, there reigned the well-fed, contented spirit of prosperity.

And then the unexpected happened. They had just sat down to the breakfast table. Though it was already eight o'clock (late breakfasts had followed naturally upon cessation of the steady work at mining) a candle in the neck of a bottle lighted the meal. Edith and Hans sat at each end of the table. On one side, with their backs to the door, sat Harkey and Dutchy. The place on the other side was vacant. Dennin had not yet come in.

Hans Nelson looked at the empty chair, shook his head slowly, and, with a ponderous attempt at humor, said: "Always is he first at the grub. It is very strange. Maybe he is sick."

"Where is Michael?" Edith asked.

"Got up a little ahead of us and went outside," Harkey answered.

Dutchy's face beamed mischievously. He pretended knowledge of Dennin's absence, and affected a mysterious air, while they clamored for information. Edith, after a peep into the men's bunk-room, returned to the table. Hans looked at her, and she shook her head.

"He was never late at meal-time before," she remarked.

"I cannot understand," said Hans. "Always has he the great appetite like the horse."

"It is too bad," Dutchy said, with a sad shake of his head.

They were beginning to make merry over their comrade's absence.

"It is a great pity!" Dutchy volunteered.

"What?" they demanded in chorus.

"Poor Michael," was the mournful reply.

"Well, what's wrong with Michael?" Harkey asked.

"He is not hungry no more," wailed Dutchy. "He has lost der appetite. He do not like der grub."

"Not from the way he pitches into it up to his ears," remarked Harkey.

"He does dot shust to be politeful to Mrs. Nelson," was Dutchy's quick retort. "I know, I know, and it is too pad. Why is he not here? Pecause he haf gone out. Why haf he gone out? For der defelopment of der appetite. How does he defelop der appetite? He walks barefoots in der snow. Ach! don't I know? It is der way der rich peoples chases after der appetite when it is no more and is running away. Michael haf sixteen hundred dollars. He is rich peoples. He haf no appetite. Derefore, pecause, he is chasing der appetite. Shust you open der door und you will see his barefoots in der snow. No, you will not see der appetite. Dot is shust his trouble. When he sees der appetite he will catch it und come to preak-fast."

They burst into loud laughter at Dutchy's nonsense. The sound had scarcely died away when the door opened and Dennin came in. All turned to look at him. He was carrying a shot-gun. Even as they looked, he lifted it to his shoulder and fired twice. At the first shot Dutchy sank upon the table, overturning his mug of coffee, his yellow mop of hair dabbling in his plate of mush. His forehead, which pressed upon the near edge of the plate, tilted the plate up against his hair at an angle of forty-five degrees. Harkey was in the air, in his spring to his feet, at the second shot, and he pitched face down upon the floor, his "My God!" gurgling and dying in his throat.

It was the unexpected. Hans and Edith were stunned. They sat at the table with bodies tense, their eyes fixed in a fascinated gaze upon the murderer. Dimly they saw him through the smoke of the powder, and in the silence nothing was to be heard save the drip-drip of Dutchy's spilled coffee on the floor. Dennin threw open the breech of the shot-gun, ejecting the empty shells. Holding the gun with one hand, he reached with the other into his pocket for fresh shells.

He was thrusting the shells into the gun when Edith Nelson was aroused to action. It was patent that he intended to kill Hans and her. For a space of possibly three seconds of time she had been dazed and paralysed by the horrible and inconceivable form in which the unexpected had made its appearance. Then she rose to it and grappled with it. She grappled with it concretely, making a cat-like leap for the murderer and gripping his neck-cloth with both her hands. The impact of her body sent him stumbling backward several steps. He tried to shake her loose and still retain his hold on the gun. This was awkward, for her firm-fleshed body had become a cat's. She threw herself to one side, and with her grip at his throat nearly jerked him to the floor. He straightened himself and whirled swiftly. Still faithful to her hold, her body followed the circle of his whirl so that her feet left the floor, and she swung through the air fastened to his throat by her hands. The whirl culminated in a collision with a chair, and the man and woman crashed to the floor in a wild struggling fall that extended itself across half the length of the room.

Hans Nelson was half a second behind his wife in rising to the unexpected. His nerve processed and mental processes were slower than hers. His was the grosser organism, and it had taken him half a second longer to perceive, and determine, and proceed to do. She had already flown at Dennin and gripped his throat, when Hans sprang to his feet. But her coolness was not his. He was in a blind fury, a Berserker rage. At the instant he sprang from his chair his mouth opened and there issued forth a sound that was half roar, half bellow. The whirl of the two bodies had already started, and still roaring, or bellowing, he pursued this whirl down the room, overtaking it when it fell to the floor.

Hans hurled himself upon the prostrate man, striking madly with his fists. They were sledge-like blows, and when Edith felt Dennin's body relax she loosed her grip and rolled clear. She lay on the floor, panting and watching. The fury of blows continued to rain down. Dennin did not seem to mind the blows. He did not even move. Then it dawned upon her that he was unconscious. She cried out to Hans to stop. She cried out again. But he paid no heed to her voice. She caught him by the arm, but her clinging to it merely impeded his effort.

It was no reasoned impulse that stirred her to do what she then did. Nor was it a sense of pity, nor obedience to the "Thou shalt not" of religion. Rather was it some sense of law, an ethic of her race and early environment, that compelled her to interpose her body between her husband and the helpless murderer. It was not until Hans knew he was striking his wife that he ceased. He allowed himself to be shoved away by her in much the same way that a ferocious but obedient dog allows itself to be shoved away by its master. The analogy went even farther. Deep in his throat, in an animal-like way, Hans's rage still rumbled, and several times he made as though to spring back upon his prey and was only prevented by the woman's swiftly interposed body.

Back and farther back Edith shoved her husband. She had never seen him in such a condition, and she was more frightened of him than she had been of Dennin in the thick of the struggle. She could not believe that this raging beast was her Hans, and with a shock she became suddenly aware of a shrinking, instinctive fear that he might snap her hand in his teeth like any wild animal. For some seconds, unwilling to hurt her, yet dogged in his desire to return to the attack, Hans dodged back and forth. But she resolutely dodged with him, until the first glimmerings of reason returned and he gave over.

Both crawled to their feet. Hans staggered back against the wall, where he leaned, his face working, in his throat the deep and continuous rumble that died away with the seconds and at last ceased. The time for the reaction had come. Edith stood in the middle of the floor, wringing her hands, panting and gasping, her whole body trembling violently.

Hans looked at nothing, but Edith's eyes wandered wildly from detail to detail of what had taken place. Dennin lay without movement. The overturned chair, hurled onward in the mad whirl, lay near him. Partly under him lay the shot-gun, still broken open at the breech. Spilling out of his right hand were the two cartridges which he had failed to put into the gun and which he had clutched until consciousness left him. Harkey lay on the floor, face downward, where he had fallen; while Dutchy rested forward on the table, his yellow mop of hair buried in his mush-plate, the plate itself still tilted at an angle of forty-five degrees. This tilted plate fascinated her. Why did it not fall down? It was ridiculous. It was not in the nature of things for a mush-plate to up-end itself on the table, even if a man or so had been killed.

She glanced back at Dennin, but her eyes returned to the tilted plate. It was so ridiculous! She felt a hysterical impulse to laugh. Then she noticed the silence, and forgot the plate in a desire for something to happen. The monotonous drip of the coffee from the table to the floor merely emphasized the silence. Why did not Hans do something? say something? She looked at him and was about to speak, when she discovered that her tongue refused its wonted duty. There was a peculiar ache in her throat, and her mouth was dry and furry. She could only look at Hans, who, in turn, looked at her.

Suddenly the silence was broken by a sharp, metallic clang. She screamed, jerking her eyes back to the table. The plate had fallen down. Hans sighed as though awakening from sleep. The clang of the plate had aroused them to life in a new world. The cabin epitomized the new world in which they must thenceforth live and move. The old cabin was gone forever. The horizon of life was totally new and unfamiliar. The unexpected had swept its wizardry over the face of things, changing the perspective, juggling values, and shuffling the real and the unreal into perplexing confusion.

"My God, Hans!" was Edith's first speech.

He did not answer, but stared at her with horror. Slowly his eyes wandered over the room, for the first time taking in its details. Then he put on his cap and started for the door.

"Where are you going?" Edith demanded, in an agony of apprehension.

His hand was on the door-knob, and he half turned as he answered, "To dig some graves."

"Don't leave me, Hans, with—" her eyes swept the room—"with this."

"The graves must be dug sometime," he said.

"But you do not know how many," she objected desperately. She noted his indecision, and added, "Besides, I'll go with you and help."

Hans stepped back to the table and mechanically snuffed the candle. Then between them they made the examination. Both Harkey and Dutchy were dead—frightfully dead, because of the close range of the shot-gun. Hans refused to go near Dennin, and Edith was forced to conduct this portion of the investigation by herself.

"He isn't dead," she called to Hans.

He walked over and looked down at the murderer.

"What did you say?" Edith demanded, having caught the rumble of inarticulate speech in her husband's throat.

"I said it was a damn shame that he isn't dead," came the reply.

Edith was bending over the body.

"Leave him alone," Hans commanded harshly, in a strange voice.

She looked at him in sudden alarm. He had picked up the shot-gun dropped by Dennin and was thrusting in the shells.

"What are you going to do?" she cried, rising swiftly from her bending position.

Hans did not answer, but she saw the shot-gun going to his shoulder. She grasped the muzzle with her hand and threw it up.

"Leave me alone!" he cried hoarsely.

He tried to jerk the weapon away from her, but she came in closer and clung to him.

"Hans! Hans! Wake up!" she cried. "Don't be crazy!"

"He killed Dutchy and Harkey!" was her husband's reply; "and I am going to kill him."

"But that is wrong," she objected. "There is the law."

He sneered his incredulity of the law's potency in such a region, but he merely iterated, dispassionately, doggedly, "He killed Dutchy and Harkey."

Long she argued it with him, but the argument was one-sided, for he contented himself with repeating again and again, "He killed Dutchy and Harkey." But she could not escape from her childhood training nor from the blood that was in her. The heritage of law was hers, and right conduct, to her, was the fulfilment of the law. She could see no other righteous course to pursue. Hans's taking the law in his own hands was no more justifiable than Dennin's deed. Two wrongs did not make a right, she contended, and there was only one way to punish Dennin, and that was the legal way arranged by society. At last Hans gave in to her.

"All right," he said. "Have it your own way. And to-morrow or next day look to see him kill you and me."

She shook her head and held out her hand for the shot-gun. He started to hand it to her, then hesitated.

"Better let me shoot him," he pleaded.

Again she shook her head, and again he started to pass her the gun, when the door opened, and an Indian, without knocking, came in. A blast of wind and flurry of snow came in with him. They turned and faced him, Hans still holding the shot-gun. The intruder took in the scene without a quiver. His eyes embraced the dead and wounded in a sweeping glance. No surprise showed in his face, not even curiosity. Harkey lay at his feet, but he took no notice of him. So far as he was concerned, Harkey's body did not exist.

"Much wind," the Indian remarked by way of salutation. "All well? Very well?"

Hans, still grasping the gun, felt sure that the Indian attributed to him the mangled corpses. He glanced appealingly at his wife.

"Good morning, Negook," she said, her voice betraying her effort. "No, not very well. Much trouble."

"Good-by, I go now, much hurry," the Indian said, and without semblance of haste, with great deliberation stepping clear of a red pool on the floor, he opened the door and went out.

The man and woman looked at each other.

"He thinks we did it," Hans gasped, "that I did it."

Edith was silent for a space. Then she said, briefly, in a businesslike way:

"Never mind what he thinks. That will come after. At present we have two graves to dig. But first of all, we've got to tie up Dennin so he can't escape."

Hans refused to touch Dennin, but Edith lashed him securely, hand and foot. Then she and Hans went out into the snow. The ground was frozen. It was impervious to a blow of the pick. They first gathered wood, then scraped the snow away and on the frozen surface built a fire. When the fire had burned for an hour, several inches of dirt had thawed. This they shovelled out, and then built a fresh fire. Their descent into the earth progressed at the rate of two or three inches an hour.

It was hard and bitter work. The flurrying snow did not permit the fire to burn any too well, while the wind cut through their clothes and chilled their bodies. They held but little conversation. The wind interfered with speech. Beyond wondering at what could have been Dennin's motive, they remained silent, oppressed by the horror of the tragedy. At one o'clock, looking toward the cabin, Hans announced that he was hungry.

"No, not now, Hans," Edith answered. "I couldn't go back alone into that cabin the way it is, and cook a meal."

At two o'clock Hans volunteered to go with her; but she held him to his work, and four o'clock found the two graves completed. They were shallow, not more than two feet deep, but they would serve the purpose. Night had fallen. Hans got the sled, and the two dead men were dragged through the darkness and storm to their frozen sepulchre. The funeral procession was anything but a pageant. The sled sank deep into the drifted snow and pulled hard. The man and the woman had eaten nothing since the previous day, and were weak from hunger and exhaustion. They had not the strength to resist the wind, and at times its buffets hurled them off their feet. On several occasions the sled was overturned, and they were compelled to reload it with its sombre freight. The last hundred feet to the graves was up a steep slope, and this they took on all fours, like sled-dogs, making legs of their arms and thrusting their hands into the snow.

Even so, they were twice dragged backward by the weight of the sled, and slid and fell down the hill, the living and the dead, the haul-ropes and the sled, in ghastly entanglement.

"To-morrow I will put up head-boards with their names," Hans said, when the graves were filled in.

Edith was sobbing. A few broken sentences had been all she was capable of in the way of a funeral service, and now her husband was compelled to half-carry her back to the cabin.

Dennin was conscious. He had rolled over and over on the floor in vain efforts to free himself. He watched Hans and Edith with glittering eyes, but made no attempt to speak. Hans still refused to touch the murderer, and sullenly watched Edith drag him across the floor to the men's bunk-room. But try as she would, she could not lift him from the floor into his bunk.

"Better let me shoot him, and we'll have no more trouble," Hans said in final appeal.

Edith shook her head and bent again to her task. To her surprise the body rose easily, and she knew Hans had relented and was helping her. Then came the cleansing of the kitchen. But the floor still shrieked the tragedy, until Hans planed the surface of the stained wood away and with the shavings made a fire in the stove.

The days came and went. There was much of darkness and silence, broken only by the storms and the thunder on the beach of the freezing surf. Hans was obedient to Edith's slightest order. All his splendid initiative had vanished. She had elected to deal with Dennin in her way, and so he left the whole matter in her hands.

The murderer was a constant menace. At all times there was the chance that he might free himself from his bonds, and they were compelled to guard him day and night. The man or the woman sat always beside him, holding the loaded shot-gun. At first, Edith tried eight-hour watches, but the continuous strain was too great, and afterwards she and Hans relieved each other every four hours. As they had to sleep, and as the watches extended through the night, their whole waking time was expended in guarding Dennin. They had barely time left over for the preparation of meals and the getting of firewood.

Since Negook's inopportune visit, the Indians had avoided the cabin. Edith sent Hans to their cabins to get them to take Dennin down the coast in a canoe to the nearest white settlement or trading post, but the errand was fruitless. Then Edith went herself and interviewed

Negook. He was head man of the little village, keenly aware of his responsibility, and he elucidated his policy thoroughly in few words.

"It is white man's trouble," he said, "not Siwash trouble. My people help you, then will it be Siwash trouble too. When white man's trouble and Siwash trouble come together and make a trouble, it is a great trouble, beyond understanding and without end. Trouble no good. My people do no wrong. What for they help you and have trouble?"

So Edith Nelson went back to the terrible cabin with its endless alternating four-hour watches. Sometimes, when it was her turn and she sat by the prisoner, the loaded shot-gun in her lap, her eyes would close and she would doze. Always she aroused with a start, snatching up the gun and swiftly looking at him. These were distinct nervous shocks, and their effect was not good on her. Such was her fear of the man, that even though she were wide awake, if he moved under the bedclothes she could not repress the start and the quick reach for the gun.

She was preparing herself for a nervous break-down, and she knew it. First came a fluttering of the eyeballs, so that she was compelled to close her eyes for relief. A little later the eyelids were afflicted by a nervous twitching that she could not control. To add to the strain, she could not forget the tragedy. She remained as close to the horror as on the first morning when the unexpected stalked into the cabin and took possession. In her daily ministrations upon the prisoner she was forced to grit her teeth and steel herself, body and spirit.

Hans was affected differently. He became obsessed by the idea that it was his duty to kill Dennin; and whenever he waited upon the bound man or watched by him, Edith was troubled by the fear that Hans would add another red entry to the cabin's record. Always he cursed Dennin savagely and handled him roughly. Hans tried to conceal his homicidal mania, and he would say to his wife: "By and by you will want me to kill him, and then I will not kill him. It would make me sick." But more than once, stealing into the room, when it was her watch off, she would catch the two men glaring ferociously at each other, wild animals the pair of them, in Hans's face the lust to kill, in Dennin's the fierceness and savagery of the cornered rat. "Hans!" she would cry, "wake up!" and he would come to a recollection of himself, startled and shamefaced and unrepentant.

So Hans became another factor in the problem the unexpected had given Edith Nelson to solve. At first it had been merely a question of right conduct in dealing with Dennin, and right conduct, as she conceived it, lay in keeping him a prisoner until he could be turned over for trial before a proper tribunal. But now entered Hans, and she saw that his sanity and his salvation were involved. Nor was she long in discovering that her own strength and endurance had become part of the problem. She was breaking down under the strain. Her left arm had developed involuntary jerkings and twitchings. She spilled her food from her spoon, and could place no reliance in her afflicted arm. She judged it to be a form of St. Vitus's dance, and she feared the extent to which its ravages might go. What if she broke down? And the vision she had of the possible future, when the cabin might contain only Dennin and Hans, was an added horror.

After the third day, Dennin had begun to talk. His first question had been, "What are you going to do with me?" And this question he repeated daily and many times a day. And always Edith replied that he would assuredly be dealt with according to law. In turn, she put a daily question to him,—"Why did you do it?" To this he never replied. Also, he received the question with out-bursts of anger, raging and straining at the rawhide that bound him and threatening her with what he would do when he got loose, which he said he was sure to do sooner or later. At such times she cocked both triggers of the gun, prepared to meet him with leaden death if he should burst loose, herself trembling and palpitating and dizzy from the tension and shock.

But in time Dennin grew more tractable. It seemed to her that he was growing weary of his unchanging recumbent position. He began to beg and plead to be released. He made wild promises. He would do them no harm. He would himself go down the coast and give himself up to the officers of the law. He would give them his share of the gold. He would go away into the heart of the wilderness, and never again appear in civilization. He would take his own life if she would only free him. His pleadings usually culminated in involuntary raving, until it seemed to her that he was passing into a fit; but always she shook her head and denied him the freedom for which he worked himself into a passion.

But the weeks went by, and he continued to grow more tractable. And through it all the weariness was asserting itself more and more. "I am so tired, so tired," he would murmur, rolling his head back and forth on the pillow like a peevish child. At a little later period he began to make impassioned pleas for death, to beg her to kill him, to beg Hans to put him our of his misery so that he might at least rest comfortably.

The situation was fast becoming impossible. Edith's nervousness was increasing, and she knew her break-down might come any time. She could not even get her proper rest, for she was haunted by the fear that Hans would yield to his mania and kill Dennin while she slept. Though January had already come, months would have to elapse before any trading schooner was even likely to put into the bay. Also, they had not expected to winter in the cabin, and the food was running low; nor could Hans add to the supply by hunting. They were chained to the cabin by the necessity of guarding their prisoner.

Something must be done, and she knew it. She forced herself to go back into a reconsideration of the problem. She could not shake off the legacy of her race, the law that was of her blood and that had been trained into her. She knew that whatever she did she must do according to the law, and in the long hours of watching, the shot-gun on her knees, the murderer restless beside her and the storms thundering without, she made original sociological researches and worked out for herself the evolution of the law. It came to her that the law was nothing more than the judgment and the will of any group of people. It mattered not how large was the group of people. There were little groups, she reasoned, like Switzerland, and there were big groups like the United States. Also, she reasoned, it did not matter how small was the group of people. There might be only ten thousand people in a country, yet their collective judgment and will would be the law of that country. Why, then, could not one thousand people constitute such a group? she asked herself. And if one thousand, why not one hundred? Why not fifty? Why not five? Why not—two?

She was frightened at her own conclusion, and she talked it over with Hans. At first he could not comprehend, and then, when he did, he added convincing evidence. He spoke of miners' meetings, where all the men of a locality came together and made the law and executed the law. There might be only ten or fifteen men altogether, he said, but the will of the majority became the law for the whole ten or fifteen, and whoever violated that will was punished.

Edith saw her way clear at last. Dennin must hang. Hans agreed with her. Between them they constituted the majority of this particular group. It was the group-will that Dennin should be hanged. In the execution of this will Edith strove earnestly to observe the customary forms, but the group was so small that Hans and she had to serve as witnesses, as jury, and as judges—also as executioners. She formally charged Michael Dennin with the murder of Dutchy and Harkey, and the prisoner lay in his bunk and listened to the testimony, first of Hans, and then of Edith. He refused to plead guilty or not guilty, and remained silent when she asked him if he had anything to say in his own defence. She and Hans, without leaving their seats, brought in the jury's verdict of guilty. Then, as judge, she imposed the sentence. Her voice shook, her eyelids twitched, her left arm jerked, but she carried it out.

"Michael Dennin, in three days' time you are to be hanged by the neck until you are dead."

Such was the sentence. The man breathed an unconscious sigh of relief, then laughed defiantly, and said, "Thin I'm thinkin' the damn bunk won't be achin' me back anny more, an' that's a consolation."

With the passing of the sentence a feeling of relief seemed to communicate itself to all of them. Especially was it noticeable in Dennin. All sullenness and defiance disappeared, and he talked sociably with his captors, and even with flashes of his old-time wit. Also, he found great satisfaction in Edith's reading to him from the Bible. She read from the New Testament, and he took keen interest in the prodigal son and the thief on the cross.

On the day preceding that set for the execution, when Edith asked her usual question, "Why did you do it?" Dennin answered, "'Tis very simple. I was thinkin'—"

But she hushed him abruptly, asked him to wait, and hurried to Hans's bedside. It was his watch off, and he came out of his sleep, rubbing his eyes and grumbling.

"Go," she told him, "and bring up Negook and one other Indian. Michael's going to confess. Make them come. Take the rifle along and bring them up at the point of it if you have to."

Half an hour later Negook and his uncle, Hadikwan, were ushered into the death chamber. They came unwillingly, Hans with his rifle herding them along.

"Negook," Edith said, "there is to be no trouble for you and your people. Only is it for you to sit and do nothing but listen and understand."

Thus did Michael Dennin, under sentence of death, make public confession of his crime. As he talked, Edith wrote his story down, while the Indians listened, and Hans guarded the door for fear the witnesses might bolt.

He had not been home to the old country for fifteen years, Dennin explained, and it had always been his intention to return with plenty of money and make his old mother comfortable for the rest of her days.

"An' how was I to be doin' it on sixteen hundred?" he demanded. "What I was after wantin' was all the goold, the whole eight thousan'. Thin I cud go back in style. What ud be aisier, thinks I to myself, than to kill all iv yez, report it at Skaguay for an Indian-killin', an' thin pull out for Ireland? An' so I started in to kill all iv yez, but, as Harkey was fond of sayin', I cut out too large a chunk an' fell down on the swallowin' iv it. An' that's me confession. I did me duty to the devil, an' now, God willin', I'll do me duty to God."

"Negook and Hadikwan, you have heard the white man's words," Edith said to the Indians. "His words are here on this paper, and it is for you to make a sign, thus, on the paper, so that white men to come after will know that you have heard."

The two Siwashes put crosses opposite their signatures, received a summons to appear on the morrow with all their tribe for a further witnessing of things, and were allowed to go.

Dennin's hands were released long enough for him to sign the document. Then a silence fell in the room. Hans was restless, and Edith felt uncomfortable. Dennin lay on his back, staring straight up at the moss-chinked roof.

"An' now I'll do me duty to God," he murmured. He turned his head toward Edith. "Read to me," he said, "from the book;" then added, with a glint of playfulness, "Mayhap 'twill help me to forget the bunk."

The day of the execution broke clear and cold. The thermometer was down to twenty-five below zero, and a chill wind was blowing which drove the frost through clothes and flesh to the bones. For the first time in many weeks Dennin stood upon his feet. His muscles had remained inactive so long, and he was so out of practice in maintaining an erect position, that he could scarcely stand.

He reeled back and forth, staggered, and clutched hold of Edith with his bound hands for support.

"Sure, an' it's dizzy I am," he laughed weakly.

A moment later he said, "An' it's glad I am that it's over with. That damn bunk would iv been the death iv me, I know."

When Edith put his fur cap on his head and proceeded to pull the flaps down over his ears, he laughed and said:

"What are you doin' that for?"

"It's freezing cold outside," she answered.

"An' in tin minutes' time what'll matter a frozen ear or so to poor Michael Dennin?" he asked.

She had nerved herself for the last culminating ordeal, and his remark was like a blow to her self-possession. So far, everything had seemed phantom-like, as in a dream, but the brutal truth of what he had said shocked her eyes wide open to the reality of what was taking place. Nor was her distress unnoticed by the Irishman.

"I'm sorry to be troublin' you with me foolish spache," he said regretfully. "I mint nothin' by it. 'Tis a great day for Michael Dennin, an' he's as gay as a lark."

He broke out in a merry whistle, which quickly became lugubrious and ceased.

"I'm wishin' there was a priest," he said wistfully; then added swiftly, "But Michael Dennin's too old a campaigner to miss the luxuries when he hits the trail."

He was so very weak and unused to walking that when the door opened and he passed outside, the wind nearly carried him off his feet. Edith and Hans walked on either side of him and supported him, the while he cracked jokes and tried to keep them cheerful, breaking off, once, long enough to arrange the forwarding of his share of the gold to his mother in Ireland.

They climbed a slight hill and came out into an open space among the trees. Here, circled solemnly about a barrel that stood on end in the snow, were Negook and Hadikwan, and all the Siwashes down to the babies and the dogs, come to see the way of the white man's law. Near by was an open grave which Hans had burned into the frozen earth.

Dennin cast a practical eye over the preparations, noting the grave, the barrel, the thickness of the rope, and the diameter of the limb over which the rope was passed.

"Sure, an' I couldn't iv done better meself, Hans, if it'd been for you."

He laughed loudly at his own sally, but Hans's face was frozen into a sullen ghastliness that nothing less than the trump of doom could have broken. Also, Hans was feeling very sick. He had not realized the enormousness of the task of putting a fellow-man out of the world. Edith, on the other hand, had realized; but the realization did not make the task any easier. She was filled with doubt as to whether she could hold herself together long enough to finish it. She felt incessant impulses to scream, to shriek, to collapse into the snow, to put her hands over her eyes and turn and run blindly away, into the forest, anywhere, away. It was only by a supreme effort of soul that she was able to keep upright and go on and do what she had to do. And in the midst of it all she was grateful to Dennin for the way he helped her.

"Lind me a hand," he said to Hans, with whose assistance he managed to mount the barrel.

He bent over so that Edith could adjust the rope about his neck. Then he stood upright while Hans drew the rope taut across the overhead branch.

"Michael Dennin, have you anything to say?" Edith asked in a clear voice that shook in spite of her.

Dennin shuffled his feet on the barrel, looked down bashfully like a man making his maiden speech, and cleared his throat.

"I'm glad it's over with," he said. "You've treated me like a Christian, an' I'm thankin' you hearty for your kindness."

"Then may God receive you, a repentant sinner," she said.

"Ay," he answered, his deep voice as a response to her thin one, "may God receive me, a repentant sinner."

"Good-by, Michael," she cried, and her voice sounded desperate.

She threw her weight against the barrel, but it did not overturn.

"Hans! Quick! Help me!" she cried faintly.

She could feel her last strength going, and the barrel resisted her. Hans hurried to her, and the barrel went out from under Michael Dennin.

She turned her back, thrusting her fingers into her ears. Then she began to laugh, harshly, sharply, metallically; and Hans was shocked as he had not been shocked through the whole tragedy. Edith Nelson's break-down had come. Even in her hysteria she knew it, and she was glad that she had been able to hold up under the strain until everything had been accomplished. She reeled toward Hans.

"Take me to the cabin, Hans," she managed to articulate.

"And let me rest," she added. "Just let me rest, and rest, and rest."

With Hans's arm around her, supporting her weight and directing her helpless steps, she went off across the snow. But the Indians remained solemnly to watch the working of the white man's law that compelled a man to dance upon the air.

JACK LONDON

# Brown Wolf

S he had delayed, because of the dew-wet grass, in order to put on her overshoes, and when she emerged from the house found her waiting husband absorbed in the wonder of a bursting almond-bud. She sent a questing glance across the tall grass and in and out among the orchard trees.

"Where's Wolf?" she asked.

"He was here a moment ago." Walt Irvine drew himself away with a jerk from the metaphysics and poetry of the organic miracle of blossom, and surveyed the landscape. "He was running a rabbit the last I saw of him."

"Wolf! Wolf! Here Wolf!" she called, as they left the clearing and took the trail that led down through the waxen-belled manzanita jungle to the county road.

Irvine thrust between his lips the little finger of each hand and lent to her efforts a shrill whistling.

She covered her ears hastily and made a wry grimace.

"My! for a poet, delicately attuned and all the rest of it, you can make unlovely noises. My ear-drums are pierced. You outwhistle—"

"Orpheus."

"I was about to say a street-arab," she concluded severely.

"Poesy does not prevent one from being practical—at least it doesn't prevent *me*. Mine is no futility of genius that can't sell gems to the magazines."

He assumed a mock extravagance, and went on:

"I am no attic singer, no ballroom warbler. And why? Because I am practical. Mine is no squalor of song that cannot transmute itself, with proper exchange value, into a flower-crowned cottage, a sweet mountain-meadow, a grove of redwoods, an orchard of thirty-seven trees, one long row of blackberries and two short rows of strawberries, to say nothing of a quarter of a mile of gurgling brook. I am a beauty-merchant, a trader in song, and I pursue utility, dear Madge. I sing a song, and thanks to the magazine editors I transmute my song into a waft of the west wind sighing through our redwoods, into a murmur of waters over mossy stones that sings back to me another song than the one I sang and yet the same song wonderfully—er—transmuted."

"O that all your song-transmutations were as successful!" she laughed.

"Name one that wasn't."

"Those two beautiful sonnets that you transmuted into the cow that was accounted the worst milker in the township."

"She was beautiful—" he began,

"But she didn't give milk," Madge interrupted.

"But she *was* beautiful, now, wasn't she?" he insisted.

"And here's where beauty and utility fall out," was her reply. "And there's the Wolf!"

From the thicket-covered hillside came a crashing of underbrush, and then, forty feet above them, on the edge of the sheer wall of rock, appeared a wolf's head and shoulders. His braced fore paws dislodged a pebble, and with sharp-pricked ears and peering eyes he watched the fall of the pebble till it struck at their feet. Then he transferred his gaze and with open mouth laughed down at them.

"You Wolf, you!" and "You blessed Wolf!" the man and woman called out to him.

The ears flattened back and down at the sound, and the head seemed to snuggle under the caress of an invisible hand.

They watched him scramble backward into the thicket, then proceeded on their way. Several minutes later, rounding a turn in the trail where the descent was less precipitous, he joined them in the midst of a miniature avalanche of pebbles and loose soil. He was not demonstrative. A pat and a rub around the ears from the man, and a more prolonged caressing from the woman, and he was away down the trail in front of them, gliding effortlessly over the ground in true wolf fashion.

In build and coat and brush he was a huge timber-wolf; but the lie was given to his wolfhood by his color and marking. There the dog unmistakably advertised itself. No wolf was ever colored like him. He was brown, deep brown, red-brown, an orgy of browns. Back and shoulders were a warm brown that paled on the sides and underneath to a yellow that was dingy because of the brown that lingered in it. The white of the throat and paws and the spots over the eyes was dirty because of the persistent and ineradicable brown, while the eyes themselves were twin topazes, golden and brown.

The man and woman loved the dog very much; perhaps this was because it had been such a task to win his love. It had been no easy matter when he first drifted in mysteriously out of nowhere to their little mountain cottage. Footsore and famished, he had killed a rabbit under their very noses and under their very windows, and then crawled away and slept by the spring at the foot of the blackberry bushes. When Walt Irvine went down to inspect the intruder, he was snarled at for his pains, and Madge likewise was snarled at when she went down to present, as a peace-offering, a large pan of bread and milk.

A most unsociable dog he proved to be, resenting all their advances, refusing to let them lay hands on him, menacing them with bared fangs and bristling hair. Nevertheless he remained, sleeping and resting by the spring, and eating the food they gave him after they set it down at a safe distance and retreated. His wretched physical condition explained why he lingered; and when he had recuperated, after several days' sojourn, he disappeared.

And this would have been the end of him, so far as Irvine and his wife were concerned, had not Irvine at that particular time been called away into the northern part of the state. Riding along on the train, near to the line between California and Oregon, he chanced to look out of the window and saw his unsociable guest sliding along the wagon road, brown and wolfish, tired yet tireless, dust-covered and soiled with two hundred miles of travel.

Now Irvine was a man of impulse, a poet. He got off the train at the next station, bought a piece of meat at a butcher shop, and captured the vagrant on the outskirts of the town. The return trip was made in the baggage car, and so Wolf came a second time to the mountain cottage. Here he was tied up for a week and made love to by the man and woman. But it was very circumspect love-making. Remote and alien as a traveller from another planet, he snarled down their soft-spoken love-words. He never barked. In all the time they had him he was never known to bark.

To win him became a problem. Irvine liked problems. He had a metal plate made, on which was stamped: *Return to Walt Irvine, Glen Ellen, Sonoma County, California*. This was riveted to a collar and strapped about the dog's neck. Then he was turned loose, and promptly he disappeared. A day later came a telegram from Mendocino County. In twenty hours he had made over a hundred miles to the north, and was still going when captured.

He came back by Wells Fargo Express, was tied up three days, and was loosed on the fourth and lost. This time he gained southern Oregon before he was caught and returned. Always, as soon as he received his liberty, he fled away, and always he fled north. He was possessed of an obsession that drove him north. The homing instinct, Irvine called it, after he had expended the selling price of a sonnet in getting the animal back from northern Oregon.

Another time the brown wanderer succeeded in traversing half the length of California, all of Oregon, and most of Washington, before he was picked up and returned "Collect." A remarkable thing was the speed with which he travelled. Fed up and rested, as soon as he was loosed he devoted all his energy to getting over the ground. On the first day's run he was known to cover as high as a hundred and fifty miles, and after that he would average a hundred miles a day until caught. He always arrived back lean and hungry and savage, and always departed fresh and vigorous, cleaving his way northward in response to some prompting of his being that no one could understand.

But at last, after a futile year of flight, he accepted the inevitable and elected to remain at the cottage where first he had killed the rabbit and slept by the spring. Even after that, a long time elapsed before the man and woman succeeded in patting him. It was a great victory, for they alone were allowed to put hands on him. He was fastidiously exclusive, and no guest at the cottage ever succeeded in making up to him. A low growl greeted such approach; if any one had the hardihood to come nearer, the lips lifted, the naked fangs appeared, and the growl became a snarl—a snarl so terrible and malignant that it awed the stoutest of them, as it likewise awed the farmers' dogs that knew ordinary dog-snarling, but had never seen wolf-snarling before.

He was without antecedents. His history began with Walt and Madge. He had come up from the south, but never a clew did they get of the owner from whom he had evidently fled. Mrs. Johnson, their nearest neighbor and the one who supplied them with milk, proclaimed him a Klondike dog. Her brother was burrowing for frozen pay-streaks in that far country, and so she constituted herself an authority on the subject.

But they did not dispute her. There were the tips of Wolf's ears, obviously so severely frozen at some time that they would never quite heal again. Besides, he looked like the photographs of the Alaskan dogs they saw published in magazines and newspapers. They often speculated over his past, and tried to conjure up (from what they had read and heard) what his northland life had been. That the northland still drew him, they knew; for at night they sometimes heard him crying softly; and when the north wind blew and the bite of frost was in the air, a great restlessness would come upon him and he would lift a mournful lament which they knew to be the long wolf-howl. Yet he never barked. No provocation was great enough to draw from him that canine cry.

Long discussion they had, during the time of winning him, as to whose dog he was. Each claimed him, and each proclaimed loudly any expression of affection made by him. But the man had the better of it at first, chiefly because he was a man. It was patent that Wolf had had no experience with women. He did not understand women. Madge's skirts were something he never quite accepted. The swish of them was enough to set him a-bristle with suspicion, and on a windy day she could not approach him at all.

On the other hand, it was Madge who fed him; also it was she who ruled the kitchen, and it was by her favor, and her favor alone, that he was permitted to come within that sacred precinct. It was because of these things that she bade fair to overcome the handicap of her garments. Then it was that Walt put forth special effort, making it a practice to have Wolf lie at his feet while he wrote, and, between petting and talking, losing much time from his work. Walt won in the end, and his victory was most probably due to the fact that he was a man, though Madge averred that they would have had another quarter of a mile of gurgling brook, and at least two west winds sighing through their redwoods, had Wait properly devoted his energies to song-transmutation and left Wolf alone to exercise a natural taste and an unbiassed judgment.

"It's about time I heard from those triolets," Walt said, after a silence of five minutes, during which they had swung steadily down the trail. "There'll be a check at the post-office, I know, and we'll transmute it into beautiful buckwheat flour, a gallon of maple syrup, and a new pair of overshoes for you."

"And into beautiful milk from Mrs. Johnson's beautiful cow," Madge added. "To-morrow's the first of the month, you know."

Walt scowled unconsciously; then his face brightened, and he clapped his hand to his breast pocket.

"Never mind. I have here a nice beautiful new cow, the best milker in California."

"When did you write it?" she demanded eagerly. Then, reproachfully, "And you never showed it to me."

"I saved it to read to you on the way to the post-office, in a spot remarkably like this one," he answered, indicating, with a wave of his hand, a dry log on which to sit.

A tiny stream flowed out of a dense fern-brake, slipped down a mossy-lipped stone, and ran across the path at their feet. From the valley arose the mellow song of meadow-larks, while about them, in and out, through sunshine and shadow, fluttered great yellow butterflies.

Up from below came another sound that broke in upon Walt reading softly from his manuscript. It was a crunching of heavy feet, punctuated now and again by the clattering of a displaced stone. As Walt finished and looked to his wife for approval, a man came into view around the turn of the trail. He was bare-headed and sweaty. With a handkerchief in one hand he mopped his face, while in the other hand he carried a new hat and a wilted starched collar which he had removed from his neck. He was a well-built man, and his muscles seemed on the point of bursting out of the painfully new and ready-made black clothes he wore.

"Warm day," Walt greeted him. Walt believed in country democracy, and never missed an opportunity to practise it.

The man paused and nodded.

"I guess I ain't used much to the warm," he vouchsafed half apologetically. "I'm more accustomed to zero weather."

"You don't find any of that in this country," Walt laughed.

"Should say not," the man answered. "An' I ain't here a-lookin' for it neither. I'm tryin' to find my sister. Mebbe you know where she lives. Her name's Johnson, Mrs. William Johnson."

"You're not her Klondike brother!" Madge cried, her eyes bright with interest, "about whom we've heard so much?"

"Yes'm, that's me," he answered modestly. "My name's Miller, Skiff Miller. I just thought I'd s'prise her."

"You are on the right track then. Only you've come by the foot-path." Madge stood up to direct him, pointing up the canyon a quarter of a mile. "You see that blasted redwood? Take the little trail turning off to the right. It's the short cut to her house. You can't miss it."

"Yes'm, thank you, ma'am," he said. He made tentative efforts to go, but seemed awkwardly rooted to the spot. He was gazing at her with an open admiration of which he was quite unconscious, and which was drowning, along with him, in the rising sea of embarrassment in which he floundered.

"We'd like to hear you tell about the Klondike," Madge said. "Mayn't we come over some day while you are at your sister's? Or, better yet, won't you come over and have dinner with us?"

"Yes'm, thank you, ma'am," he mumbled mechanically. Then he caught himself up and added: "I ain't stoppin' long. I got to be pullin' north again. I go out on to-night's train. You see, I've got a mail contract with the government."

When Madge had said that it was too bad, he made another futile effort to go. But he could not take his eyes from her face. He forgot his embarrassment in his admiration, and it was her turn to flush and feel uncomfortable.

It was at this juncture, when Walt had just decided it was time for him to be saying something to relieve the strain, that Wolf, who had been away nosing through the brush, trotted wolf-like into view.

Skiff Miller's abstraction disappeared. The pretty woman before him passed out of his field of vision. He had eyes only for the dog, and a great wonder came into his face.

"Well, I'll be damned!" he enunciated slowly and solemnly.

He sat down ponderingly on the log, leaving Madge standing. At the sound of his voice, Wolf's ears had flattened down, then his mouth had opened in a laugh. He trotted slowly up to the stranger and first smelled his hands, then licked them with his tongue.

Skiff Miller patted the dog's head, and slowly and solemnly repeated, "Well, I'll be damned!"

"Excuse me, ma'am," he said the next moment "I was just s'prised some, that was all."

"We're surprised, too," she answered lightly. "We never saw Wolf make up to a stranger before."

"Is that what you call him—Wolf?" the man asked.

Madge nodded. "But I can't understand his friendliness toward you—unless it's because you're from the Klondike. He's a Klondike dog, you know."

"Yes'm," Miller said absently. He lifted one of Wolf's fore legs and examined the foot-pads, pressing them and denting them with his thumb. "Kind of soft," he remarked. "He ain't been on trail for a long time."

"I say," Walt broke in, "it is remarkable the way he lets you handle him."

Skiff Miller arose, no longer awkward with admiration of Madge, and in a sharp, businesslike manner asked, "How long have you had him?"

But just then the dog, squirming and rubbing against the newcomer's legs, opened his mouth and barked. It was an explosive bark, brief and joyous, but a bark.

"That's a new one on me," Skiff Miller remarked.

Walt and Madge stared at each other. The miracle had happened. Wolf had barked.

"It's the first time he ever barked," Madge said.

"First time I ever heard him, too," Miller volunteered.

Madge smiled at him. The man was evidently a humorist.

"Of course," she said, "since you have only seen him for five minutes."

Skiff Miller looked at her sharply, seeking in her face the guile her words had led him to suspect.

"I thought you understood," he said slowly. "I thought you'd tumbled to it from his makin' up to me. He's my dog. His name ain't Wolf. It's Brown."

"Oh, Walt!" was Madge's instinctive cry to her husband.

Walt was on the defensive at once.

"How do you know he's your dog?" he demanded.

"Because he is," was the reply.

"Mere assertion," Walt said sharply.

In his slow and pondering way, Skiff Miller looked at him, then asked, with a nod of his head toward Madge:

"How d'you know she's your wife? You just say, 'Because she is,' and I'll say it's mere assertion. The dog's mine. I bred 'm an' raised 'm, an' I guess I ought to know. Look here. I'll prove it to you."

Skiff Miller turned to the dog. "Brown!" His voice rang out sharply, and at the sound the dog's ears flattened down as to a caress. "Gee!" The dog made a swinging turn to the right. "Now mush-on!" And the dog ceased his swing abruptly and started straight ahead, halting obediently at command.

"I can do it with whistles," Skiff Miller said proudly. "He was my lead dog."

"But you are not going to take him away with you?" Madge asked tremulously.

The man nodded.

"Back into that awful Klondike world of suffering?"

He nodded and added: "Oh, it ain't so bad as all that. Look at me. Pretty healthy specimen, ain't I?"

"But the dogs! The terrible hardship, the heart-breaking toil, the starvation, the frost! Oh, I've read about it and I know."

"I nearly ate him once, over on Little Fish River," Miller volunteered grimly. "If I hadn't got a moose that day was all that saved 'm."

"I'd have died first!" Madge cried.

"Things is different down here," Miller explained. "You don't have to eat dogs. You think different just about the time you're all in. You've never ben all in, so you don't know anything about it."

"That's the very point," she argued warmly. "Dogs are not eaten in California. Why not leave him here? He is happy. He'll never want for food—you know that. He'll never suffer from cold and hardship. Here all is softness and gentleness. Neither the human nor nature is savage. He will never know a whip-lash again. And as for the weather—why, it never snows here."

"But it's all-fired hot in summer, beggin' your pardon," Skiff Miller laughed.

"But you do not answer," Madge continued passionately. "What have you to offer him in that northland life?"

"Grub, when I've got it, and that's most of the time," came the answer.

"And the rest of the time?"

"No grub."

"And the work?"

"Yes, plenty of work," Miller blurted out impatiently. "Work without end, an' famine, an' frost, an all the rest of the miseries—that's what he'll get when he comes with me. But he likes it. He is used to it. He knows that life. He was born to it an' brought up to it. An' you don't know anything about it. You don't know what you're talking about. That's where the dog belongs, and that's where he'll be happiest."

"The dog doesn't go," Walt announced in a determined voice. "So there is no need of further discussion."

"What's that?" Skiff Miller demanded, his brows lowering and an obstinate flush of blood reddening his forehead.

"I said the dog doesn't go, and that settles it. I don't believe he's your dog. You may have seen him sometime. You may even sometime have driven him for his owner. But his obeying the ordinary driving commands of the Alaskan trail is no demonstration that he is yours. Any dog in Alaska would obey you as he obeyed. Besides, he is undoubtedly a valuable dog, as dogs go in Alaska, and that is sufficient explanation of your desire to get possession of him. Anyway, you've got to prove property."

Skiff Miller, cool and collected, the obstinate flush a trifle deeper on his forehead, his huge muscles bulging under the black cloth of his coat, carefully looked the poet up and down as though measuring the strength of his slenderness.

The Klondiker's face took on a contemptuous expression as he said finally, "I reckon there's nothin' in sight to prevent me takin' the dog right here an' now."

Walt's face reddened, and the striking-muscles of his arms and shoulders seemed to stiffen and grow tense. His wife fluttered apprehensively into the breach.

"Maybe Mr. Miller is right," she said. "I am afraid that he is. Wolf does seem to know him, and certainly he answers to the name of 'Brown.' He made friends with him instantly, and you know that's something he never did with anybody before. Besides, look at the way he barked. He was just bursting with joy. Joy over what? Without doubt at finding Mr. Miller."

Walt's striking-muscles relaxed, and his shoulders seemed to droop with hopelessness.

"I guess you're right, Madge," he said. "Wolf isn't Wolf, but Brown, and he must belong to Mr. Miller."

"Perhaps Mr. Miller will sell him," she suggested. "We can buy him."

Skiff Miller shook his head, no longer belligerent, but kindly, quick to be generous in response to generousness.

"I had five dogs," he said, casting about for the easiest way to temper his refusal. "He was the leader. They was the crack team of Alaska. Nothin' could touch 'em. In 1898 I refused five thousand dollars for the bunch. Dogs was high, then, anyway; but that wasn't what made the fancy price. It was the team itself. Brown was the best in the team. That winter I refused twelve hundred for 'm. I didn't sell 'm then, an' I ain't a-sellin' 'm now. Besides, I think a mighty lot of that dog. I've ben lookin' for 'm for three years. It made me fair sick when I found he'd ben stole—not the value of him, but the—well, I liked 'm like hell, that's all, beggin' your pardon. I couldn't believe my eyes when I seen 'm just now. I thought I was dreamin'. It was too good to be true. Why, I was his wet-nurse. I put 'm to bed, snug every night. His mother died, and I brought 'm up on condensed milk at two dollars a can when I couldn't afford it in my own coffee. He never knew any mother but me. He used to suck my finger regular, the darn little cuss—that finger right there!"

And Skiff Miller, too overwrought for speech, held up a fore finger for them to see.

"That very finger," he managed to articulate, as though it somehow clinched the proof of ownership and the bond of affection.

He was still gazing at his extended finger when Madge began to speak.

"But the dog," she said. "You haven't considered the dog."

Skiff Miller looked puzzled.

"Have you thought about him?" she asked.

"Don't know what you're drivin' at," was the response.

"Maybe the dog has some choice in the matter," Madge went on. "Maybe he has his likes and desires. You have not considered him. You give him no choice. It has never entered your mind that possibly he might prefer California to Alaska. You consider only what you like. You do with him as you would with a sack of potatoes or a bale of hay."

This was a new way of looking at it, and Miller was visibly impressed as he debated it in his mind. Madge took advantage of his indecision.

"If you really love him, what would be happiness to him would be your happiness also," she urged.

Skiff Miller continued to debate with himself, and Madge stole a glance of exultation to her husband, who looked back warm approval.

"What do you think?" the Klondiker suddenly demanded.

It was her turn to be puzzled. "What do you mean?" she asked.

"D'ye think he'd sooner stay in California?"

She nodded her head with positiveness. "I am sure of it."

Skiff Miller again debated with himself, though this time aloud, at the same time running his gaze in a judicial way over the mooted animal.

"He was a good worker. He's done a heap of work for me. He never loafed on me, an' he was a joe-dandy at hammerin' a raw team into shape. He's got a head on him. He can do everything but talk. He knows what you say to him. Look at 'm now. He knows we're talkin' about him."

The dog was lying at Skiff Miller's feet, head close down on paws, ears erect and listening, and eyes that were quick and eager to follow the sound of speech as it fell from the lips of first one and then the other.

"An' there's a lot of work in 'm yet. He's good for years to come. An' I do like him. I like him like hell."

Once or twice after that Skiff Miller opened his mouth and closed it again without speaking. Finally he said:

"I'll tell you what I'll do. Your remarks, ma'am, has some weight in them. The dog's worked hard, and maybe he's earned a soft berth an' has got a right to choose. Anyway, we'll leave it up to him. Whatever he says, goes. You people stay right here settin' down. I'll say good-by and walk off casual-like. If he wants to stay, he can stay. If he wants to come with me, let 'm come. I won't call 'm to come an' don't you call 'm to come back."

He looked with sudden suspicion at Madge, and added, "Only you must play fair. No persuadin' after my back is turned."

"We'll play fair," Madge began, but Skiff Miller broke in on her assurances.

"I know the ways of women," he announced. "Their hearts is soft. When their hearts is touched they're likely to stack the cards, look at the bottom of the deck, an' lie like the devil—beggin' your pardon, ma'am. I'm only discoursin' about women in general."

"I don't know how to thank you," Madge quavered.

"I don't see as you've got any call to thank me," he replied. "Brown ain't decided yet. Now you won't mind if I go away slow? It's no more'n fair, seein' I'll be out of sight inside a hundred yards."—Madge agreed, and added, "And I promise you faithfully that we won't do anything to influence him."

"Well, then, I might as well be gettin' along," Skiff Miller said in the ordinary tones of one departing.

At this change in his voice, Wolf lifted his head quickly, and still more quickly got to his feet when the man and woman shook hands. He sprang up on his hind legs, resting his fore paws on her hip and at the same time licking Skiff Miller's hand. When the latter shook hands with Walt, Wolf repeated his act, resting his weight on Walt and licking both men's hands.

"It ain't no picnic, I can tell you that," were the Klondiker's last words, as he turned and went slowly up the trail.

For the distance of twenty feet Wolf watched him go, himself all eagerness and expectancy, as though waiting for the man to turn and retrace his steps. Then, with a quick low whine, Wolf sprang after him, overtook him, caught his hand between his teeth with reluctant tenderness, and strove gently to make him pause.

Failing in this, Wolf raced back to where Walt Irvine sat, catching his coat-sleeve in his teeth and trying vainly to drag him after the retreating man.

Wolf's perturbation began to wax. He desired ubiquity. He wanted to be in two places at the same time, with the old master and the new, and steadily the distance between them was increasing. He sprang about excitedly, making short nervous leaps and twists, now toward one, now toward the other, in painful indecision, not knowing his own mind, desiring both and unable to choose, uttering quick sharp whines and beginning to pant.

He sat down abruptly on his haunches, thrusting his nose upward, the mouth opening and closing with jerking movements, each time opening wider. These jerking movements were in unison with the recurrent spasms that attacked the throat, each spasm severer and more intense than the preceding one. And in accord with jerks and spasms the larynx began to vibrate, at first silently, accompanied by the rush of air expelled from the lungs, then sounding a low, deep note, the lowest in the register of the human ear. All this was the nervous and muscular preliminary to howling.

But just as the howl was on the verge of bursting from the full throat, the wide-opened mouth was closed, the paroxysms ceased, and he looked long and steadily at the retreating man. Suddenly Wolf turned his head, and over his shoulder just as steadily regarded Walt. The appeal was unanswered. Not a word nor a sign did the dog receive, no suggestion and no clew as to what his conduct should be.

A glance ahead to where the old master was nearing the curve of the trail excited him again. He sprang to his feet with a whine, and then, struck by a new idea, turned his attention to Madge. Hitherto he had ignored her, but now, both masters failing him, she alone was left. He went over to her and snuggled his head in her lap, nudging her arm with his nose—an old trick of his when begging for favors. He backed away from her and began writhing and twisting playfully, curvetting and prancing, half rearing and striking his fore paws to the earth, struggling with all his body, from the wheedling eyes and flattening ears to the wagging tail, to express the thought that was in him and that was denied him utterance.

This, too, he soon abandoned. He was depressed by the coldness of these humans who had never been cold before. No response could he draw from them, no help could he get. They did not consider him. They were as dead.

He turned and silently gazed after the old master. Skiff Miller was rounding the curve. In a moment he would be gone from view. Yet he never turned his head, plodding straight onward, slowly and methodically, as though possessed of no interest in what was occurring behind his back.

And in this fashion he went out of view. Wolf waited for him to reappear. He waited a long minute, silently, quietly, without movement, as though turned to stone—withal stone quick with eagerness and desire. He barked once, and waited. Then he turned and trotted back to Walt Irvine. He sniffed his hand and dropped down heavily at his feet, watching the trail where it curved emptily from view.

The tiny stream slipping down the mossy-lipped stone seemed suddenly to increase the volume of its gurgling noise. Save for the meadow-larks, there was no other sound. The great yellow butterflies drifted silently through the sunshine and lost themselves in the drowsy shadows. Madge gazed triumphantly at her husband.

A few minutes later Wolf got upon his feet. Decision and deliberation marked his movements. He did not glance at the man and woman. His eyes were fixed up the trail. He had made up his mind. They knew it. And they knew, so far as they were concerned, that the ordeal had just begun.

He broke into a trot, and Madge's lips pursed, forming an avenue for the caressing sound that it was the will of her to send forth. But the caressing sound was not made. She was impelled to look at her husband, and she saw the sternness with which he watched her. The pursed lips relaxed, and she sighed inaudibly.

Wolf's trot broke into a run. Wider and wider were the leaps he made. Not once did he turn his head, his wolf's brush standing out straight behind him. He cut sharply across the curve of the trail and was gone.

# The Sun-Dog Trail

Sitka Charley smoked his pipe and gazed thoughtfully at the *Police Gazette* illustration on the wall. For half an hour he had been steadily regarding it, and for half an hour I had been slyly watching him. Something was going on in that mind of his, and, whatever it was, I knew it was well worth knowing. He had lived life, and seen things, and performed that prodigy of prodigies, namely, the turning of his back upon his own people, and, in so far as it was possible for an Indian, becoming a white man even in his mental processes. As he phrased it himself, he had come into the warm, sat among us, by our fires, and become one of us. He had never learned to read nor write, but his vocabulary was remarkable, and more remarkable still was the completeness with which he had assumed the white man's point of view, the white man's attitude toward things.

We had struck this deserted cabin after a hard day on trail. The dogs had been fed, the supper dishes washed, the beds made, and we were now enjoying that most delicious hour that comes each day, and but once each day, on the Alaskan trail, the hour when nothing intervenes between the tired body and bed save the smoking of the evening pipe. Some former denizen of the cabin had decorated its walls with illustrations torn from magazines and newspapers, and it was these illustrations that had held Sitka Charley's attention from the moment of our arrival two hours before. He had studied them intently, ranging from one to another and back again, and I could see that there was uncertainty in his mind, and bepuzzlement.

"Well?" I finally broke the silence.

He took the pipe from his mouth and said simply, "I do not understand."

He smoked on again, and again removed the pipe, using it to point at the *Police Gazette* illustration.

"That picture—what does it mean? I do not understand."

I looked at the picture. A man, with a preposterously wicked face, his right hand pressed dramatically to his heart, was falling backward to the floor. Confronting him, with a face that was a composite of destroying angel and Adonis, was a man holding a smoking revolver.

"One man is killing the other man," I said, aware of a distinct bepuzzlement of my own and of failure to explain.

"Why?" asked Sitka Charley.

"I do not know," I confessed.

"That picture is all end," he said. "It has no beginning."

"It is life," I said.

"Life has beginning," he objected.

I was silenced for the moment, while his eyes wandered on to an adjoining decoration, a photographic reproduction of somebody's "Leda and the Swan."

"That picture," he said, "has no beginning. It has no end. I do not understand pictures."

"Look at that picture," I commanded, pointing to a third decoration. "It means something. Tell me what it means to you."

He studied it for several minutes.

"The little girl is sick," he said finally. "That is the doctor looking at her. They have been up all night—see, the oil is low in the lamp, the first morning light is coming in at the window. It is a great sickness; maybe she will die, that is why the doctor looks so hard. That is the mother. It is a great sickness, because the mother's head is on the table and she is crying."

"How do you know she is crying?" I interrupted. "You cannot see her face. Perhaps she is asleep."

Sitka Charley looked at me in swift surprise, then back at the picture. It was evident that he had not reasoned the impression.

"Perhaps she is asleep," he repeated. He studied it closely. "No, she is not asleep. The shoulders show that she is not asleep. I have seen the shoulders of a woman who cried. The mother is crying. It is a very great sickness."

"And now you understand the picture," I cried.

He shook his head, and asked, "The little girl—does it die?"

It was my turn for silence.

"Does it die?" he reiterated. "You are a painter-man. Maybe you know."

"No, I do not know," I confessed.

"It is not life," he delivered himself dogmatically. "In life little girl die or get well. Something happen in life. In picture nothing happen. No, I do not understand pictures."

His disappointment was patent. It was his desire to understand all things that white men understand, and here, in this matter, he failed. I felt, also, that there was challenge in his attitude. He was bent upon compelling me to show him the wisdom of pictures. Besides, he had remarkable powers of visualization. I had long since learned this. He visualized everything. He saw life in pictures, felt life in pictures, generalized life in pictures; and yet he did not understand pictures when seen through other men's eyes and expressed by those men with color and line upon canvas.

"Pictures are bits of life," I said. "We paint life as we see it. For instance, Charley, you are coming along the trail. It is night. You see a cabin. The window is lighted. You look through the window for one second, or for two seconds, you see something, and you go on your way. You saw maybe a man writing a letter. You saw something without beginning or end. Nothing happened. Yet it was a bit of life you saw. You remember it afterward. It is like a picture in your memory. The window is the frame of the picture."

I could see that he was interested, and I knew that as I spoke he had looked through the window and seen the man writing the letter.

"There is a picture you have painted that I understand," he said. "It is a true picture. It has much meaning. It is in your cabin at Dawson. It is a faro table. There are men playing. It is a large game. The limit is off."

"How do you know the limit is off?" I broke in excitedly, for here was where my work could be tried out on an unbiassed judge who knew life only, and not art, and who was a sheer master of reality. Also, I was very proud of that particular piece of work. I had named it "The Last Turn," and I believed it to be one of the best things I had ever done.

"There are no chips on the table," Sitka Charley explained. "The men are playing with markers. That means the roof is the limit. One man play yellow markers—maybe one yellow marker worth one thousand dollars, maybe two thousand dollars. One man play red markers. Maybe they are worth five hundred dollars, maybe one thousand dollars. It is a very big game. Everybody play very high, up to the roof. How do I know? You make the dealer with blood little bit warm in face." (I was delighted.) "The lookout, you make him lean forward in his chair. Why he lean forward? Why his face very much quiet? Why his eyes very much bright? Why dealer warm with blood a little bit in the face? Why all men very quiet?—the man with yellow markers? the man with white markers? the man with red markers? Why nobody talk? Because very much money. Because last turn."

"How do you know it is the last turn?" I asked.

"The king is coppered, the seven is played open," he answered. "Nobody bet on other cards. Other cards all gone. Everybody one mind.

Everybody play king to lose, seven to win. Maybe bank lose twenty thousand dollars, maybe bank win. Yes, that picture I understand."

"Yet you do not know the end!" I cried triumphantly. "It is the last turn, but the cards are not yet turned. In the picture they will never be turned. Nobody will ever know who wins nor who loses."

"And the men will sit there and never talk," he said, wonder and awe growing in his face. "And the lookout will lean forward, and the blood will be warm in the face of the dealer. It is a strange thing. Always will they sit there, always; and the cards will never be turned."

"It is a picture," I said. "It is life. You have seen things like it yourself."

He looked at me and pondered, then said, very slowly: "No, as you say, there is no end to it. Nobody will ever know the end. Yet is it a true thing. I have seen it. It is life."

For a long time he smoked on in silence, weighing the pictorial wisdom of the white man and verifying it by the facts of life. He nodded his head several times, and grunted once or twice. Then he knocked the ashes from his pipe, carefully refilled it, and after a thoughtful pause, lighted it again.

"Then have I, too, seen many pictures of life," he began; "pictures not painted, but seen with the eyes. I have looked at them like through the window at the man writing the letter. I have seen many pieces of life, without beginning, without end, without understanding."

With a sudden change of position he turned his eyes full upon me and regarded me thoughtfully.

"Look you," he said; "you are a painter-man. How would you paint this which I saw, a picture without beginning, the ending of which I do not understand, a piece of life with the northern lights for a candle and Alaska for a frame."

"It is a large canvas," I murmured.

But he ignored me, for the picture he had in mind was before his eyes and he was seeing it.

"There are many names for this picture," he said. "But in the picture there are many sun-dogs, and it comes into my mind to call it 'The Sun-Dog Trail.' It was a long time ago, seven years ago, the fall of '97, when I saw the woman first time. At Lake Linderman I had one canoe, very good Peterborough canoe. I came over Chilcoot Pass with two thousand letters for Dawson. I was letter carrier. Everybody rush to Klondike at that time. Many people on trail. Many people chop down trees and make boats. Last water, snow in the air, snow on the ground, ice on the lake, on the river ice in the eddies. Every day more snow, more ice. Maybe one day, maybe three days, maybe six days, any day maybe freeze-up come, then no more water, all ice, everybody walk, Dawson six hundred miles, long time walk. Boat go very quick. Everybody want to go boat. Everybody say, 'Charley, two hundred dollars you take me in canoe,' 'Charley, three hundred dollars,' 'Charley, four hundred dollars.' I say no, all the time I say no. I am letter carrier.

"In morning I get to Lake Linderman. I walk all night and am much tired. I cook breakfast, I eat, then I sleep on the beach three hours. I wake up. It is ten o'clock. Snow is falling. There is wind, much wind that blows fair. Also, there is a woman who sits in the snow alongside. She is white woman, she is young, very pretty, maybe she is twenty years old, maybe twenty-five years old. She look at me. I look at her. She is very tired. She is no dance-woman. I see that right away. She is good woman, and she is very tired.

"'You are Sitka Charley,' she says. I get up quick and roll blankets so snow does not get inside. 'I go to Dawson,' she says. 'I go in your canoe—how much?'

"I do not want anybody in my canoe. I do not like to say no. So I say, 'One thousand dollars.' Just for fun I say it, so woman cannot come with me, much better than say no. She look at me very hard, then she says, 'When you start?' I say right away. Then she says all right, she will give me one thousand dollars.

"What can I say? I do not want the woman, yet have I given my word that for one thousand dollars she can come. I am surprised. Maybe she make fun, too, so I say, 'Let me see thousand dollars.' And that woman, that young woman, all alone on the trail, there in the snow, she take out one thousand dollars, in greenbacks, and she put them in my hand. I look at money, I look at her. What can I say? I say, 'No, my canoe very small. There is no room for outfit.' She laugh. She says, 'I am great traveller. This is my outfit.' She kick one small pack in the snow. It is two fur robes, canvas outside, some woman's clothes inside. I pick it up. Maybe thirty-five pounds. I am surprised. She take it away from me. She says, 'Come, let us start.' She carries pack into canoe. What can I say? I put my blankets into canoe. We start.

"And that is the way I saw the woman first time. The wind was fair. I put up small sail. The canoe went very fast, it flew like a bird over the high waves. The woman was much afraid. 'What for you come Klondike much afraid?' I ask. She laugh at me, a hard laugh, but she is still much afraid. Also is she very tired. I run canoe through rapids to Lake Bennett. Water very bad, and woman cry out because she is afraid. We go down Lake Bennett, snow, ice, wind like a gale, but woman is very tired and go to sleep.

"That night we make camp at Windy Arm. Woman sit by fire and eat supper. I look at her. She is pretty. She fix hair. There is much hair, and it is brown, also sometimes it is like gold in the firelight, when she turn her head, so, and flashes come from it like golden fire. The eyes are large and brown, sometimes warm like a candle behind a curtain, sometimes very hard and bright like broken ice when sun shines upon it. When she smile—how can I say?—when she smile I know white man like to kiss her, just like that, when she smile. She never do hard work. Her hands are soft, like baby's hand. She is soft all over, like baby. She is not thin, but round like baby; her arm, her leg, her muscles, all soft and round like baby. Her waist is small, and when she stand up, when she walk, or move her head or arm, it is—I do not know the word—but it is nice to look at, like—maybe I say she is built on lines like the lines of a good canoe, just like that, and when she move she is like the movement of the good canoe sliding through still water or leaping through water when it is white and fast and angry. It is very good to see.

"Why does she come into Klondike, all alone, with plenty of money? I do not know. Next day I ask her. She laugh and says: 'Sitka Charley, that is none of your business. I give you one thousand dollars take me to Dawson. That only is your business.' Next day after that I ask her what is her name. She laugh, then she says, 'Mary Jones, that is my name.' I do not know her name, but I know all the time that Mary Jones is not her name.

"It is very cold in canoe, and because of cold sometimes she not feel good. Sometimes she feel good and she sing. Her voice is like a silver bell, and I feel good all over like when I go into church at Holy Cross Mission, and when she sing I feel strong and paddle like hell. Then she laugh and says, 'You think we get to Dawson before freeze-up, Charley?' Sometimes she sit in canoe and is thinking far away, her eyes like that, all empty. She does not see Sitka Charley, nor the ice, nor the snow. She is far away. Very often she is like that, thinking far away. Sometimes, when she is thinking far away, her face is not good to see. It looks like a face that is angry, like the face of one man when he want to kill another man.

"Last day to Dawson very bad. Shore-ice in all the eddies, mush-ice in the stream. I cannot paddle. The canoe freeze to ice. I cannot get to shore. There is much danger. All the time we go down Yukon in the ice. That night there is much noise of ice. Then ice stop, canoe stop, everything stop. 'Let us go to shore,' the woman says. I say no, better wait. By and by, everything start down-stream again. There is much snow. I cannot see. At eleven o'clock at night, everything stop. At one o'clock everything start again. At three o'clock everything stop. Canoe is smashed like eggshell, but is on top of ice and cannot sink. I hear dogs howling. We wait. We sleep. By and by morning come. There is no more snow. It is the freeze-up, and there is Dawson. Canoe smash and stop right at Dawson. Sitka Charley has come in with two thousand letters on very last water.

"The woman rent a cabin on the hill, and for one week I see her no more. Then, one day, she come to me. 'Charley,' she says, 'how do you like to work for me? You drive dogs, make camp, travel with me.' I say that I make too much money carrying letters. She says, 'Charley, I will pay you more money.' I tell her that pick-and-shovel man get fifteen dollars a day in the mines. She says, 'That is four hundred and fifty dollars a month.' And I say, 'Sitka Charley is no pick-and-shovel man.' Then she says, 'I understand, Charley. I will give you seven hundred and fifty dollars each month.' It is a good price, and I go to work for her. I buy for her dogs and sled. We travel up Klondike, up Bonanza and Eldorado, over to Indian River, to Sulphur Creek, to Dominion, back across divide to Gold Bottom and to Too Much Gold, and back to Dawson. All the time she look for something, I do not know what. I am puzzled. 'What thing you look for?' I ask. She laugh. 'You look for gold?' I ask. She laugh. Then she says, 'That is none of your business, Charley.' And after that I never ask any more.

"She has a small revolver which she carries in her belt. Sometimes, on trail, she makes practice with revolver. I laugh. 'What for you laugh, Charley?' she ask. 'What for you play with that?' I say. 'It is no good. It is too small. It is for a child, a little plaything.' When we get back to Dawson she ask me to buy good revolver for her. I buy a Colt's 44. It is very heavy, but she carry it in her belt all the time.

"At Dawson comes the man. Which way he come I do not know. Only do I know he is *checha-quo*—what you call tenderfoot. His hands are soft, just like hers. He never do hard work. He is soft all over. At first I think maybe he is her husband. But he is too young. Also, they make two beds at night. He is maybe twenty years old. His eyes blue, his hair yellow, he has a little mustache which is yellow. His name is

John Jones. Maybe he is her brother. I do not know. I ask questions no more. Only I think his name not John Jones. Other people call him Mr. Girvan. I do not think that is his name. I do not think her name is Miss Girvan, which other people call her. I think nobody know their names.

"One night I am asleep at Dawson. He wake me up. He says, 'Get the dogs ready; we start.' No more do I ask questions, so I get the dogs ready and we start. We go down the Yukon. It is night-time, it is November, and it is very cold—sixty-five below. She is soft. He is soft. The cold bites. They get tired. They cry under their breaths to themselves. By and by I say better we stop and make camp. But they say that they will go on. Three times I say better to make camp and rest, but each time they say they will go on. After that I say nothing. All the time, day after day, is it that way. They are very soft. They get stiff and sore. They do not understand moccasins, and their feet hurt very much. They limp, they stagger like drunken people, they cry under their breaths; and all the time they say, 'On! on! We will go on!'

"They are like crazy people. All the time do they go on, and on. Why do they go on? I do not know. Only do they go on. What are they after? I do not know. They are not after gold. There is no stampede. Besides, they spend plenty of money. But I ask questions no more. I, too, go on and on, because I am strong on the trail and because I am greatly paid.

"We make Circle City. That for which they look is not there. I think now that we will rest, and rest the dogs. But we do not rest, not for one day do we rest. 'Come,' says the woman to the man, 'let us go on.' And we go on. We leave the Yukon. We cross the divide to the west and swing down into the Tanana Country. There are new diggings there. But that for which they look is not there, and we take the back trail to Circle City.

"It is a hard journey. December is most gone. The days are short. It is very cold. One morning it is seventy below zero. 'Better that we don't travel to-day,' I say, 'else will the frost be unwarmed in the breathing and bite all the edges of our lungs. After that we will have bad cough, and maybe next spring will come pneumonia.' But they are *checha-quo*. They do not understand the trail. They are like dead people they are so tired, but they say, 'Let us go on.' We go on. The frost bites their lungs, and they get the dry cough. They cough till the tears run down their cheeks. When bacon is frying they must run away from the fire and cough half an hour in the snow. They freeze their cheeks a little bit, so that the skin turns black and is very sore. Also, the man freezes his thumb till the end is like to come off, and he must wear a large thumb on his mitten to keep it warm. And sometimes, when the frost bites hard and the thumb is very cold, he must take off the mitten and put the hand between his legs next to the skin, so that the thumb may get warm again.

"We limp into Circle City, and even I, Sitka Charley, am tired. It is Christmas Eve. I dance, drink, make a good time, for to-morrow is Christmas Day and we will rest. But no. It is five o'clock in the morning—Christmas morning. I am two hours asleep. The man stand by my bed. 'Come, Charley,' he says, 'harness the dogs. We start.'

"Have I not said that I ask questions no more? They pay me seven hundred and fifty dollars each month. They are my masters. I am their man. If they say, 'Charley, come, let us start for hell,' I will harness the dogs, and snap the whip, and start for hell. So I harness the dogs, and we start down the Yukon. Where do we go? They do not say. Only do they say, 'On! on! We will go on!'

"They are very weary. They have travelled many hundreds of miles, and they do not understand the way of the trail. Besides, their cough is very bad—the dry cough that makes strong men swear and weak men cry. But they go on. Every day they go on. Never do they rest the dogs. Always do they buy new dogs. At every camp, at every post, at every Indian village, do they cut out the tired dogs and put in fresh dogs. They have much money, money without end, and like water they spend it. They are crazy? Sometimes I think so, for there is a devil in them that drives them on and on, always on. What is it that they try to find? It is not gold. Never do they dig in the ground. I think a long time. Then I think it is a man they try to find. But what man? Never do we see the man. Yet are they like wolves on the trail of the kill. But they are funny wolves, soft wolves, baby wolves who do not understand the way of the trail. They cry aloud in their sleep at night. In their sleep they moan and groan with the pain of their weariness. And in the day, as they stagger along the trail, they cry under their breaths. They are funny wolves.

"We pass Fort Yukon. We pass Fort Hamilton. We pass Minook. January has come and nearly gone. The days are very short. At nine o'clock comes daylight. At three o'clock comes night. And it is cold. And even I, Sitka Charley, am tired. Will we go on forever this way without end? I do not know. But always do I look along the trail for that which they try to find. There are few people on the trail. Sometimes we travel one hundred miles and never see a sign of life. It is very quiet. There is no sound. Sometimes it snows, and we are like wandering ghosts. Sometimes it is clear, and at midday the sun looks at us for a moment over the hills to the south. The northern lights flame in the sky, and the sun-dogs dance, and the air is filled with frost-dust.

"I am Sitka Charley, a strong man. I was born on the trail, and all my days have I lived on the trail. And yet have these two baby wolves made me very tired. I am lean, like a starved cat, and I am glad of my bed at night, and in the morning am I greatly weary. Yet ever are we hitting the trail in the dark before daylight, and still on the trail does the dark after nightfall find us. These two baby wolves! If I am lean like a starved cat, they are lean like cats that have never eaten and have died. Their eyes are sunk deep in their heads, bright sometimes as with fever, dim and cloudy sometimes like the eyes of the dead. Their cheeks are hollow like caves in a cliff. Also are their cheeks black and raw from many freezings. Sometimes it is the woman in the morning who says, 'I cannot get up. I cannot move. Let me die.' And it is the man who stands beside her and says, 'Come, let us go on.' And they go on. And sometimes it is the man who cannot get up, and the woman says, 'Come, let us go on.' But the one thing they do, and always do, is to go on. Always do they go on.

"Sometimes, at the trading posts, the man and woman get letters. I do not know what is in the letters. But it is the scent that they follow, these letters themselves are the scent. One time an Indian gives them a letter. I talk with him privately. He says it is a man with one eye who gives him the letter, a man who travels fast down the Yukon. That is all. But I know that the baby wolves are after the man with the one eye.

"It is February, and we have travelled fifteen hundred miles. We are getting near Bering Sea, and there are storms and blizzards. The going is hard. We come to Anvig. I do not know, but I think sure they get a letter at Anvig, for they are much excited, and they say, 'Come, hurry, let us go on.' But I say we must buy grub, and they say we must travel light and fast. Also, they say that we can get grub at Charley McKeon's cabin. Then do I know that they take the big cut-off, for it is there that Charley McKeon lives where the Black Rock stands by the trail.

"Before we start, I talk maybe two minutes with the priest at Anvig. Yes, there is a man with one eye who has gone by and who travels fast.

And I know that for which they look is the man with the one eye. We leave Anvig with little grub, and travel light and fast. There are three fresh dogs bought in Anvig, and we travel very fast. The man and woman are like mad. We start earlier in the morning, we travel later at night. I look sometimes to see them die, these two baby wolves, but they will not die. They go on and on. When the dry cough take hold of them hard, they hold their hands against their stomach and double up in the snow, and cough, and cough, and cough. They cannot walk, they cannot talk. Maybe for ten minutes they cough, maybe for half an hour, and then they straighten up, the tears from the coughing frozen on their faces, and the words they say are, 'Come, let us go on.'

"Even I, Sitka Charley, am greatly weary, and I think seven hundred and fifty dollars is a cheap price for the labor I do. We take the big cut-off, and the trail is fresh. The baby wolves have their noses down to the trail, and they say, 'Hurry!' All the time do they say, 'Hurry! Faster! Faster!' It is hard on the dogs. We have not much food and we cannot give them enough to eat, and they grow weak. Also, they must work hard. The woman has true sorrow for them, and often, because of them, the tears are in her eyes. But the devil in her that drives her on will not let her stop and rest the dogs.

"And then we come upon the man with the one eye. He is in the snow by the trail, and his leg is broken. Because of the leg he has made a poor camp, and has been lying on his blankets for three days and keeping a fire going. When we find him he is swearing. He swears like hell. Never have I heard a man swear like that man. I am glad. Now that they have found that for which they look, we will have rest. But the woman says, 'Let us start. Hurry!'

"I am surprised. But the man with the one eye says, 'Never mind me. Give me your grub. You will get more grub at McKeon's cabin tomorrow. Send McKeon back for me. But do you go on.' Here is another wolf, an old wolf, and he, too, thinks but the one thought, to go on. So we give him our grub, which is not much, and we chop wood for his fire, and we take his strongest dogs and go on. We left the man with one eye there in the snow, and he died there in the snow, for McKeon never went back for him. And who that man was, and why he came to be there, I do not know. But I think he was greatly paid by the man and the woman, like me, to do their work for them.

"That day and that night we had nothing to eat, and all next day we travelled fast, and we were weak with hunger. Then we came to the

Black Rock, which rose five hundred feet above the trail. It was at the end of the day. Darkness was coming, and we could not find the cabin of McKeon. We slept hungry, and in the morning looked for the cabin. It was not there, which was a strange thing, for everybody knew that McKeon lived in a cabin at Black Rock. We were near to the coast, where the wind blows hard and there is much snow. Everywhere there were small hills of snow where the wind had piled it up. I have a thought, and I dig in one and another of the hills of snow. Soon I find the walls of the cabin, and I dig down to the door. I go inside. McKeon is dead. Maybe two or three weeks he is dead. A sickness had come upon him so that he could not leave the cabin. The wind and the snow had covered the cabin. He had eaten his grub and died. I looked for his cache, but there was no grub in it.

"'Let us go on,' said the woman. Her eyes were hungry, and her hand was upon her heart, as with the hurt of something inside. She bent back and forth like a tree in the wind as she stood there. 'Yes, let us go on,' said the man. His voice was hollow, like the *klonk* of an old raven, and he was hunger-mad. His eyes were like live coals of fire, and as his body rocked to and fro, so rocked his soul inside. And I, too, said, 'Let us go on.' For that one thought, laid upon me like a lash for every mile of fifteen hundred miles, had burned itself into my soul, and I think that I, too, was mad. Besides, we could only go on, for there was no grub. And we went on, giving no thought to the man with the one eye in the snow.

"There is little travel on the big cut-off. Sometimes two or three months and nobody goes by. The snow had covered the trail, and there was no sign that men had ever come or gone that way. All day the wind blew and the snow fell, and all day we travelled, while our stomachs gnawed their desire and our bodies grew weaker with every step they took. Then the woman began to fall. Then the man. I did not fall, but my feet were heavy and I caught my toes and stumbled many times.

"That night is the end of February. I kill three ptarmigan with the woman's revolver, and we are made somewhat strong again. But the dogs have nothing to eat. They try to eat their harness, which is of leather and walrus-hide, and I must fight them off with a club and hang all the harness in a tree. And all night they howl and fight around that tree. But we do not mind. We sleep like dead people, and in the morning get up like dead people out of their graves and go on along the trail.

"That morning is the 1st of March, and on that morning I see the first sign of that after which the baby wolves are in search. It is clear weather, and cold. The sun stay longer in the sky, and there are sun-dogs flashing on either side, and the air is bright with frost-dust. The snow falls no more upon the trail, and I see the fresh sign of dogs and sled. There is one man with that outfit, and I see in the snow that he is not strong. He, too, has not enough to eat. The young wolves see the fresh sign, too, and they are much excited. 'Hurry!' they say. All the time they say, 'Hurry! Faster, Charley, faster!'

"We make hurry very slow. All the time the man and the woman fall down. When they try to ride on sled the dogs are too weak, and the dogs fall down. Besides, it is so cold that if they ride on the sled they will freeze. It is very easy for a hungry man to freeze. When the woman fall down, the man help her up. Sometimes the woman help the man up. By and by both fall down and cannot get up, and I must help them up all the time, else they will not get up and will die there in the snow. This is very hard work, for I am greatly weary, and as well I must drive the dogs, and the man and woman are very heavy with no strength in their bodies. So, by and by, I, too, fall down in the snow, and there is no one to help me up. I must get up by myself. And always do I get up by myself, and help them up, and make the dogs go on.

"That night I get one ptarmigan, and we are very hungry. And that night the man says to me, 'What time start to-morrow, Charley?' It is like the voice of a ghost. I say, 'All the time you make start at five o'clock.' 'To-morrow,' he says, 'we will start at three o'clock.' I laugh in great bitterness, and I say, 'You are dead man.' And he says, 'To-morrow we will start at three o'clock.'

"And we start at three o'clock, for I am their man, and that which they say is to be done, I do. It is clear and cold, and there is no wind. When daylight comes we can see a long way off. And it is very quiet. We can hear no sound but the beat of our hearts, and in the silence that is a very loud sound. We are like sleep-walkers, and we walk in dreams until we fall down; and then we know we must get up, and we see the trail once more and bear the beating of our hearts. Sometimes, when I am walking in dreams this way, I have strange thoughts. Why does Sitka Charley live? I ask myself. Why does Sitka Charley work hard, and go hungry, and have all this pain? For seven hundred and fifty dollars a month, I make the answer, and I know it is a foolish answer. Also is it a true answer. And after that never again do I care for money. For that day a large wisdom came to me. There was a great light, and I saw clear, and I knew that it was not for money that a man must live, but for a happiness that no man can give, or buy, or sell, and that is beyond all value of all money in the world.

"In the morning we come upon the last-night camp of the man who is before us. It is a poor camp, the kind a man makes who is hungry and without strength. On the snow there are pieces of blanket and of canvas, and I know what has happened. His dogs have eaten their harness, and he has made new harness out of his blankets. The man and woman stare hard at what is to be seen, and as I look at them my back feels the chill as of a cold wind against the skin. Their eyes are toil-mad and hunger-mad, and burn like fire deep in their heads. Their faces are like the faces of people who have died of hunger, and their cheeks are black with the dead flesh of many freezings. 'Let us go on,' says the man. But the woman coughs and falls in the snow. It is the dry cough where the frost has bitten the lungs. For a long time she coughs, then like a woman crawling out of her grave she crawls to her feet. The tears are ice upon her cheeks, and her breath makes a noise as it comes and goes, and she says, 'Let us go on.'

"We go on. And we walk in dreams through the silence. And every time we walk is a dream and we are without pain; and every time we fall down is an awakening, and we see the snow and the mountains and the fresh trail of the man who is before us, and we know all our pain again. We come to where we can see a long way over the snow, and that for which they look is before them. A mile away there are black spots upon the snow. The black spots move. My eyes are dim, and I must stiffen my soul to see. And I see one man with dogs and a sled. The baby wolves see, too. They can no longer talk, but they whisper, 'On, on. Let us hurry!'

"And they fall down, but they go on. The man who is before us, his blanket harness breaks often, and he must stop and mend it. Our harness is good, for I have hung it in trees each night. At eleven o'clock the man is half a mile away. At one o'clock he is a quarter of a mile away. He is very weak. We see him fall down many times in the snow. One of his dogs can no longer travel, and he cuts it out of the harness. But he does not kill it. I kill it with the axe as I go by, as I kill one of my dogs which loses its legs and can travel no more.

"Now we are three hundred yards away. We go very slow. Maybe in two, three hours we go one mile. We do not walk. All the time we fall down. We stand up and stagger two steps, maybe three steps, then we fall down again. And all the time I must help up the man and woman.

Sometimes they rise to their knees and fall forward, maybe four or five times before they can get to their feet again and stagger two or three steps and fall. But always do they fall forward. Standing or kneeling, always do they fall forward, gaining on the trail each time by the length of their bodies.

"Sometimes they crawl on hands and knees like animals that live in the forest. We go like snails, like snails that are dying we go so slow. And yet we go faster than the man who is before us. For he, too, falls all the time, and there is no Sitka Charley to lift him up. Now he is two hundred yards away. After a long time he is one hundred yards away.

"It is a funny sight. I want to laugh out loud, Ha! ha! just like that, it is so funny. It is a race of dead men and dead dogs. It is like in a dream when you have a nightmare and run away very fast for your life and go very slow. The man who is with me is mad. The woman is mad. I am mad. All the world is mad, and I want to laugh, it is so funny.

"The stranger-man who is before us leaves his dogs behind and goes on alone across the snow. After a long time we come to the dogs. They lie helpless in the snow, their harness of blanket and canvas on them, the sled behind them, and as we pass them they whine to us and cry like babies that are hungry.

"Then we, too, leave our dogs and go on alone across the snow. The man and the woman are nearly gone, and they moan and groan and sob, but they go on. I, too, go on. I have but one thought. It is to come up to the stranger-man. Then it is that I shall rest, and not until then shall I rest, and it seems that I must lie down and sleep for a thousand years, I am so tired.

"The stranger-man is fifty yards away, all alone in the white snow. He falls and crawls, staggers, and falls and crawls again. He is like an animal that is sore wounded and trying to run from the hunter. By and by he crawls on hands and knees. He no longer stands up. And the man and woman no longer stand up. They, too, crawl after him on hands and knees. But I stand up. Sometimes I fall, but always do I stand up again.

"It is a strange thing to see. All about is the snow and the silence, and through it crawl the man and the woman, and the stranger-man who goes before. On either side the sun are sun-dogs, so that there are three suns in the sky. The frost-dust is like the dust of diamonds, and all the air is filled with it. Now the woman coughs, and lies still in the snow until the fit has passed, when she crawls on again. Now the man looks ahead, and he is blear-eyed as with old age and must rub his eyes so that he can see the stranger-man. And now the stranger-man looks back over his shoulder. And Sitka Charley, standing upright, maybe falls down and stands upright again.

"After a long time the stranger-man crawls no more. He stands slowly upon his feet and rocks back and forth. Also does he take off one mitten and wait with revolver in his hand, rocking back and forth as he waits. His face is skin and bones and frozen black. It is a hungry face. The eyes are deep-sunk in his head, and the lips are snarling. The man and woman, too, get upon their feet and they go toward him very slowly. And all about is the snow and the silence. And in the sky are three suns, and all the air is flashing with the dust of diamonds.

"And thus it was that I, Sitka Charley, saw the baby wolves make their kill. No word is spoken. Only does the stranger-man snarl with his hungry face. Also does he rock to and fro, his shoulders drooping, his knees bent, and his legs wide apart so that he does not fall down. The man and the woman stop maybe fifty feet away. Their legs, too, are wide apart so that they do not fall down, and their bodies rock to and fro. The stranger-man is very weak. His arm shakes, so that when he shoots at the man his bullet strikes in the snow. The man cannot take off his mitten. The stranger-man shoots at him again, and this time the bullet goes by in the air. Then the man takes the mitten in his teeth and pulls it off. But his hand is frozen and he cannot hold the revolver, and it fails in the snow. I look at the woman. Her mitten is off, and the big Colt's revolver is in her hand. Three times she shoot, quick, just like that. The hungry face of the stranger-man is still snarling as he falls forward into the snow.

"They do not look at the dead man. 'Let us go on,' they say. And we go on. But now that they have found that for which they look, they are like dead. The last strength has gone out of them. They can stand no more upon their feet. They will not crawl, but desire only to close their eyes and sleep. I see not far away a place for camp. I kick them. I have my dog-whip, and I give them the lash of it. They cry aloud, but they must crawl. And they do crawl to the place for camp. I build fire so that they will not freeze. Then I go back for sled. Also, I kill the dogs of the stranger-man so that we may have food and not die. I put the man and woman in blankets and they sleep. Sometimes I wake them and give them little bit of food. They are not awake, but they take the food. The woman sleep one day and a half. Then she wake up and go to sleep again. The man sleep two days and wake up and go to sleep again.

After that we go down to the coast at St. Michaels. And when the ice goes out of Bering Sea, the man and woman go away on a steamship. But first they pay me my seven hundred and fifty dollars a month. Also, they make me a present of one thousand dollars. And that was the year that Sitka Charley gave much money to the Mission at Holy Cross."

"But why did they kill the man?" I asked.

Sitka Charley delayed reply until he had lighted his pipe. He glanced at the *Police Gazette* illustration and nodded his head at it familiarly. Then he said, speaking slowly and ponderingly:

"I have thought much. I do not know. It is something that happened. It is a picture I remember. It is like looking in at the window and seeing the man writing a letter. They came into my life and they went out of my life, and the picture is as I have said, without beginning, the end without understanding."

"You have painted many pictures in the telling," I said.

"Ay," he nodded his head. "But they were without beginning and without end."

"The last picture of all had an end," I said.

"Ay," he answered. "But what end?"

"It was a piece of life," I said.

"Ay," he answered. "It was a piece of life."

# Negore, the Coward

He had followed the trail of his fleeing people for eleven days, and his pursuit had been in itself a flight; for behind him he knew full well were the dreaded Russians, toiling through the swampy lowlands and over the steep divides, bent on no less than the extermination of all his people. He was travelling light. A rabbit-skin sleeping-robe, a muzzle-loading rifle, and a few pounds of sun-dried salmon constituted his outfit. He would have marvelled that a whole people—women and children and aged—could travel so swiftly, had he not known the terror that drove them on.

It was in the old days of the Russian occupancy of Alaska, when the nineteenth century had run but half its course, that Negore fled after his fleeing tribe and came upon it this summer night by the head waters of the Pee-lat. Though near the midnight hour, it was bright day as he passed through the weary camp. Many saw him, all knew him, but few and cold were the greetings he received.

"Negore, the Coward," he heard Illiha, a young woman, laugh, and Sun-ne, his sister's daughter, laughed with her.

Black anger ate at his heart; but he gave no sign, threading his way among the camp-fires until he came to one where sat an old man. A young woman was kneading with skilful fingers the tired muscles of his legs. He raised a sightless face and listened intently as Negore's foot crackled a dead twig.

"Who comes?" he queried in a thin, tremulous voice.

"Negore," said the young woman, scarcely looking up from her task.

Negore's face was expressionless. For many minutes he stood and waited. The old man's head had sunk back upon his chest. The young woman pressed and prodded the wasted muscles, resting her body on her knees, her bowed head hidden as in a cloud by her black wealth of hair. Negore watched the supple body, bending at the hips as a lynx's body might bend, pliant as a young willow stalk, and, withal, strong as only youth is strong. He looked, and was aware of a great yearning, akin in sensation to physical hunger. At last he spoke, saying:

"Is there no greeting for Negore, who has been long gone and has but now come back?"

She looked up at him with cold eyes. The old man chuckled to himself after the manner of the old.

"Thou art my woman, Oona," Negore said, his tones dominant and conveying a hint of menace.

She arose with catlike ease and suddenness to her full height, her eyes flashing, her nostrils quivering like a deer's.

"I was thy woman to be, Negore, but thou art a coward; the daughter of Old Kinoos mates not with a coward!"

She silenced him with an imperious gesture as he strove to speak.

"Old Kinoos and I came among you from a strange land. Thy people took us in by their fires and made us warm, nor asked whence or why we wandered. It was their thought that Old Kinoos had lost the sight of his eyes from age; nor did Old Kinoos say otherwise, nor did I, his daughter. Old Kinoos is a brave man, but Old Kinoos was never a boaster. And now, when I tell thee of how his blindness came to be, thou wilt know, beyond question, that the daughter of Kinoos cannot mother the children of a coward such as thou art, Negore."

Again she silenced the speech that rushed up to his tongue.

"Know, Negore, if journey be added unto journey of all thy journeyings through this land, thou wouldst not come to the unknown Sitka on the Great Salt Sea. In that place there be many Russian folk, and their rule is harsh. And from Sitka, Old Kinoos, who was Young Kinoos in those days, fled away with me, a babe in his arms, along the islands in the midst of the sea. My mother dead tells the tale of his wrong; a Russian, dead with a spear through breast and back, tells the tale of the vengeance of Kinoos.

"But wherever we fled, and however far we fled, always did we find the hated Russian folk. Kinoos was unafraid, but the sight of them was a hurt to his eyes; so we fled on and on, through the seas and years, till we came to the Great Fog Sea, Negore, of which thou hast heard, but which thou hast never seen. We lived among many peoples, and I grew to be a woman; but Kinoos, growing old, took to him no other woman, nor did I take a man.

"At last we came to Pastolik, which is where the Yukon drowns itself in the Great Fog Sea. Here we lived long, on the rim of the sea, among a people by whom the Russians were well hated. But sometimes they came, these Russians, in great ships, and made the people of Pastolik show them the way through the islands uncountable of the many-mouthed Yukon. And sometimes the men they took to show them the way never came back, till the people became angry and planned a great plan.

"So, when there came a ship, Old Kinoos stepped forward and said he would show the way. He was an old man then, and his hair was white; but he was unafraid. And he was cunning, for he took the ship to where the sea sucks in to the land and the waves beat white on the mountain called Romanoff. The sea sucked the ship in to where the waves beat white, and it ground upon the rocks and broke open its sides. Then came all the people of Pastolik, (for this was the plan), with their war-spears, and arrows, and some few guns. But first the Russians put out the eyes of Old Kinoos that he might never show the way again, and then they fought, where the waves beat white, with the people of Pastolik.

"Now the head-man of these Russians was Ivan. He it was, with his two thumbs, who drove out the eyes of Kinoos. He it was who fought his way through the white water, with two men left of all his men, and went away along the rim of the Great Fog Sea into the north. Kinoos was wise. He could see no more and was helpless as a child. So he fled away from the sea, up the great, strange Yukon, even to Nulato, and I fled with him.

"This was the deed my father did, Kinoos, an old man. But how did the young man, Negore?"

Once again she silenced him.

"With my own eyes I saw, at Nulato, before the gates of the great fort, and but few days gone. I saw the Russian, Ivan, who thrust out my father's eyes, lay the lash of his dog-whip upon thee and beat thee like a dog. This I saw, and knew thee for a coward. But I saw thee not, that night, when all thy people—yea, even the boys not yet hunters—fell upon the Russians and slew them all."

"Not Ivan," said Negore, quietly. "Even now is he on our heels, and with him many Russians fresh up from the sea."

Oona made no effort to hide her surprise and chagrin that Ivan was not dead, but went on:

"In the day I saw thee a coward; in the night, when all men fought, even the boys not yet hunters, I saw thee not and knew thee doubly a coward."

"Thou art done? All done?" Negore asked.

She nodded her head and looked at him askance, as though astonished that he should have aught to say.

"Know then that Negore is no coward," he said; and his speech was very low and quiet. "Know that when I was yet a boy I journeyed alone down to the place where the Yukon drowns itself in the Great Fog Sea.

Even to Pastolik I journeyed, and even beyond, into the north, along the rim of the sea. This I did when I was a boy, and I was no coward. Nor was I coward when I journeyed, a young man and alone, up the Yukon farther than man had ever been, so far that I came to another folk, with white faces, who live in a great fort and talk speech other than that the Russians talk. Also have I killed the great bear of the Tanana country, where no one of my people hath ever been. And I have fought with the Nuklukyets, and the Kaltags, and the Sticks in far regions, even I, and alone. These deeds, whereof no man knows, I speak for myself. Let my people speak for me of things I have done which they know. They will not say Negore is a coward."

He finished proudly, and proudly waited.

"These be things which happened before I came into the land," she said, "and I know not of them. Only do I know what I know, and I know I saw thee lashed like a dog in the day; and in the night, when the great fort flamed red and the men killed and were killed, I saw thee not. Also, thy people do call thee Negore, the Coward. It is thy name now, Negore, the Coward."

"It is not a good name," Old Kinoos chuckled.

"Thou dost not understand, Kinoos," Negore said gently. "But I shall make thee understand. Know that I was away on the hunt of the bear, with Kamo-tah, my mother's son. And Kamo-tah fought with a great bear. We had no meat for three days, and Kamo-tah was not strong of arm nor swift of foot. And the great bear crushed him, so, till his bones cracked like dry sticks. Thus I found him, very sick and groaning upon the ground. And there was no meat, nor could I kill aught that the sick man might eat.

"So I said, 'I will go to Nulato and bring thee food, also strong men to carry thee to camp.' And Kamo-tah said, 'Go thou to Nulato and get food, but say no word of what has befallen me. And when I have eaten, and am grown well and strong, I will kill this bear. Then will I return in honor to Nulato, and no man may laugh and say Kamo-tah was undone by a bear.'

"So I gave heed to my brother's words; and when I was come to Nulato, and the Russian, Ivan, laid the lash of his dog-whip upon me, I knew I must not fight. For no man knew of Kamo-tah, sick and groaning and hungry; and did I fight with Ivan, and die, then would my brother die, too. So it was, Oona, that thou sawest me beaten like a dog.

"Then I heard the talk of the shamans and chiefs that the Russians had brought strange sicknesses upon the people, and killed our men, and stolen our women, and that the land must be made clean. As I say, I heard the talk, and I knew it for good talk, and I knew that in the night the Russians were to be killed. But there was my brother, Kamo-tah, sick and groaning and with no meat; so I could not stay and fight with the men and the boys not yet hunters.

"And I took with me meat and fish, and the lash-marks of Ivan, and I found Kamo-tah no longer groaning, but dead. Then I went back to Nulato, and, behold, there was no Nulato—only ashes where the great fort had stood, and the bodies of many men. And I saw the Russians come up the Yukon in boats, fresh from the sea, many Russians; and I saw Ivan creep forth from where he lay hid and make talk with them. And the next day I saw Ivan lead them upon the trail of the tribe. Even now are they upon the trail, and I am here, Negore, but no coward."

"This is a tale I hear," said Oona, though her voice was gentler than before. "Kamo-tah is dead and cannot speak for thee, and I know only what I know, and I must know thee of my own eyes for no coward."

Negore made an impatient gesture.

"There be ways and ways," she added. "Art thou willing to do no less than what Old Kinoos hath done?"

He nodded his head, and waited.

"As thou hast said, they seek for us even now, these Russians. Show them the way, Negore, even as Old Kinoos showed them the way, so that they come, unprepared, to where we wait for them, in a passage up the rocks. Thou knowest the place, where the wall is broken and high. Then will we destroy them, even Ivan. When they cling like flies to the wall, and top is no less near than bottom, our men shall fall upon them from above and either side, with spears, and arrows, and guns. And the women and children, from above, shall loosen the great rocks and hurl them down upon them. It will be a great day, for the Russians will be killed, the land will be made clean, and Ivan, even Ivan who thrust out my father's eyes and laid the lash of his dog-whip upon thee, will be killed. Like a dog gone mad will he die, his breath crushed out of him beneath the rocks. And when the fighting begins, it is for thee, Negore, to crawl secretly away so that thou be not slain."

"Even so," he answered. "Negore will show them the way. And then?"

"And then I shall be thy woman, Negore's woman, the brave man's woman. And thou shalt hunt meat for me and Old Kinoos, and I shall cook thy food, and sew thee warm parkas and strong, and make thee moccasins after the way of my people, which is a better way than thy people's way. And as I say, I shall be thy woman, Negore, always thy woman. And I shall make thy life glad for thee, so that all thy days will be a song and laughter, and thou wilt know the woman Oona as unlike all other women, for she has journeyed far, and lived in strange places, and is wise in the ways of men and in the ways they may be made glad. And in thine old age will she still make thee glad, and thy memory of her in the days of thy strength will be sweet, for thou wilt know always that she was ease to thee, and peace, and rest, and that beyond all women to other men has she been woman to thee."

"Even so," said Negore, and the hunger for her ate at his heart, and his arms went out for her as a hungry man's arms might go out for food.

"When thou hast shown the way, Negore," she chided him; but her eyes were soft, and warm, and he knew she looked upon him as woman had never looked before.

"It is well," he said, turning resolutely on his heel. "I go now to make talk with the chiefs, so that they may know I am gone to show the Russians the way."

"Oh, Negore, my man! my man!" she said to herself, as she watched him go, but she said it so softly that even Old Kinoos did not hear, and his ears were over keen, what of his blindness.

THREE DAYS LATER, HAVING WITH craft ill-concealed his hiding-place, Negore was dragged forth like a rat and brought before Ivan—"Ivan the Terrible" he was known by the men who marched at his back. Negore was armed with a miserable bone-barbed spear, and he kept his rabbit-skin robe wrapped closely about him, and though the day was warm he shivered as with an ague. He shook his head that he did not understand the speech Ivan put at him, and made that he was very weary and sick, and wished only to sit down and rest, pointing the while to his stomach in sign of his sickness, and shivering fiercely. But Ivan had with him a man from Pastolik who talked the speech of Negore, and many and vain were the questions they asked him concerning his tribe, till the man from Pastolik, who was called Karduk, said:

"It is the word of Ivan that thou shalt be lashed till thou diest if thou dost not speak. And know, strange brother, when I tell thee the word of Ivan is the law, that I am thy friend and no friend of Ivan. For I come not willingly from my country by the sea, and I desire greatly to live; wherefore I obey the will of my master—as thou wilt obey, strange brother, if thou art wise, and wouldst live."

"Nay, strange brother," Negore answered, "I know not the way my people are gone, for I was sick, and they fled so fast my legs gave out from under me, and I fell behind."

Negore waited while Karduk talked with Ivan. Then Negore saw the Russian's face go dark, and he saw the men step to either side of him, snapping the lashes of their whips. Whereupon he betrayed a great fright, and cried aloud that he was a sick man and knew nothing, but would tell what he knew. And to such purpose did he tell, that Ivan gave the word to his men to march, and on either side of Negore marched the men with the whips, that he might not run away. And when he made that he was weak of his sickness, and stumbled and walked not so fast as they walked, they laid their lashes upon him till he screamed with pain and discovered new strength. And when Karduk told him all would he well with him when they had overtaken his tribe, he asked, "And then may I rest and move not?"

Continually he asked, "And then may I rest and move not?"

And while he appeared very sick and looked about him with dull eyes, he noted the fighting strength of Ivan's men, and noted with satisfaction that Ivan did not recognize him as the man he had beaten before the gates of the fort. It was a strange following his dull eyes saw. There were Slavonian hunters, fair-skinned and mighty-muscled; short, squat Finns, with flat noses and round faces; Siberian half-breeds, whose noses were more like eagle-beaks; and lean, slant-eyed men, who bore in their veins the Mongol and Tartar blood as well as the blood of the Slav. Wild adventurers they were, forayers and destroyers from the far lands beyond the Sea of Bering, who blasted the new and unknown world with fire and sword and clutched greedily for its wealth of fur and hide. Negore looked upon them with satisfaction, and in his mind's eye he saw them crushed and lifeless at the passage up the rocks. And ever he saw, waiting for him at the passage up the rocks, the face and the form of Oona, and ever he heard her voice in his ears and felt the soft, warm glow of her eyes. But never did he forget to shiver, nor to stumble where the footing was rough, nor to cry aloud at the bite of the lash. Also, he was afraid of Karduk, for he knew him for no true man. His was a false eye, and an easy tongue—a tongue too easy, he judged, for the awkwardness of honest speech.

All that day they marched. And on the next, when Karduk asked him at command of Ivan, he said he doubted they would meet with his tribe till the morrow. But Ivan, who had once been shown the way by Old Kinoos, and had found that way to lead through the white water and a deadly fight, believed no more in anything. So when they came to a passage up the rocks, he halted his forty men, and through Karduk demanded if the way were clear.

Negore looked at it shortly and carelessly. It was a vast slide that broke the straight wall of a cliff, and was overrun with brush and creeping plants, where a score of tribes could have lain well hidden.

He shook his head. "Nay, there be nothing there," he said. "The way is clear."

Again Ivan spoke to Karduk, and Karduk said:

"Know, strange brother, if thy talk be not straight, and if thy people block the way and fall upon Ivan and his men, that thou shalt die, and at once."

"My talk is straight," Negore said. "The way is clear."

Still Ivan doubted, and ordered two of his Slavonian hunters to go up alone. Two other men he ordered to the side of Negore. They placed their guns against his breast and waited. All waited. And Negore knew, should one arrow fly, or one spear be flung, that his death would come upon him. The two Slavonian hunters toiled upward till they grew small and smaller, and when they reached the top and waved their hats that all was well, they were like black specks against the sky.

The guns were lowered from Negore's breast and Ivan gave the order for his men to go forward. Ivan was silent, lost in thought. For an hour he marched, as though puzzled, and then, through Karduk's mouth, he said to Negore:

"How didst thou know the way was clear when thou didst look so briefly upon it?"

Negore thought of the little birds he had seen perched among the rocks and upon the bushes, and smiled, it was so simple; but he shrugged his shoulders and made no answer. For he was thinking, likewise, of another passage up the rocks, to which they would soon come, and where the little birds would all be gone. And he was glad that Karduk came from the Great Fog Sea, where there were no trees or bushes, and where men learned water-craft instead of land-craft and wood-craft.

Three hours later, when the sun rode overhead, they came to another passage up the rocks, and Karduk said:

"Look with all thine eyes, strange brother, and see if the way be clear, for Ivan is not minded this time to wait while men go up before."

Negore looked, and he looked with two men by his side, their guns resting against his breast. He saw that the little birds were all gone, and once he saw the glint of sunlight on a rifle-barrel. And he thought of Oona, and of her words: "And when the fighting begins, it is for thee, Negore, to crawl secretly away so that thou be not slain."

He felt the two guns pressing on his breast. This was not the way she had planned. There would be no crawling secretly away. He would be the first to die when the fighting began. But he said, and his voice was steady, and he still feigned to see with dull eyes and to shiver from his sickness:

"The way is clear."

And they started up, Ivan and his forty men from the far lands beyond the Sea of Bering. And there was Karduk, the man from Pastolik, and Negore, with the two guns always upon him. It was a long climb, and they could not go fast; but very fast to Negore they seemed to approach the midway point where top was no less near than bottom.

A gun cracked among the rocks to the right, and Negore heard the war-yell of all his tribe, and for an instant saw the rocks and bushes bristle alive with his kinfolk. Then he felt torn asunder by a burst of flame hot through his being, and as he fell he knew the sharp pangs of life as it wrenches at the flesh to be free.

But he gripped his life with a miser's clutch and would not let it go. He still breathed the air, which bit his lungs with a painful sweetness; and dimly he saw and heard, with passing spells of blindness and deafness, the flashes of sight and sound again wherein he saw the hunters of Ivan falling to their deaths, and his own brothers fringing the carnage and filling the air with the tumult of their cries and weapons, and, far above, the women and children loosing the great rocks that leaped like things alive and thundered down.

The sun danced above him in the sky, the huge walls reeled and swung, and still he heard and saw dimly. And when the great Ivan fell across his legs, hurled there lifeless and crushed by a down-rushing rock, he remembered the blind eyes of Old Kinoos and was glad.

Then the sounds died down, and the rocks no longer thundered past, and he saw his tribespeople creeping close and closer, spearing the wounded as they came. And near to him he heard the scuffle of a mighty Slavonian hunter, loath to die, and, half uprisen, borne back and down by the thirsty spears.

Then he saw above him the face of Oona, and felt about him the arms of Oona; and for a moment the sun steadied and stood still, and the great walls were upright and moved not.

"Thou art a brave man, Negore," he heard her say in his ear; "thou art my man, Negore."

And in that moment he lived all the life of gladness of which she had told him, and the laughter and the song, and as the sun went out of the sky above him, as in his old age, he knew the memory of her was sweet. And as even the memories dimmed and died in the darkness that fell upon him, he knew in her arms the fulfilment of all the ease and rest she had promised him. And as black night wrapped around him, his head upon her breast, he felt a great peace steal about him, and he was aware of the hush of many twilights and the mystery of silence.

# A Note About the Author

Jack London (1876–1916) was an American novelist and journalist. Born in San Francisco to Florence Wellman, a spiritualist, and William Chaney, an astrologer, London was raised by his mother and her husband, John London, in Oakland. An intelligent boy, Jack went on to study at the University of California, Berkeley before leaving school to join the Klondike Gold Rush. His experiences in the Klondike—hard labor, life in a hostile environment, and bouts of scurvy—both shaped his sociopolitical outlook and served as powerful material for such works as "To Build a Fire" (1902), *The Call of the Wild* (1903), and *White Fang* (1906). When he returned to Oakland, London embarked on a career as a professional writer, finding success with novels and short fiction. In 1904, London worked as a war correspondent covering the Russo-Japanese War and was arrested several times by Japanese authorities. Upon returning to California, he joined the famous Bohemian Club, befriending such members as Ambrose Bierce and John Muir. London married Charmian Kittredge in 1905, the same year he purchased the thousand-acre Beauty Ranch in Sonoma County, California. London, who suffered from numerous illnesses throughout his life, died on his ranch at the age of 40. A lifelong advocate for socialism and animal rights, London is recognized as a pioneer of science fiction and an important figure in twentieth century American literature.

# A Note from the Publisher

Spanning many genres, from non-fiction essays to literature classics to children's books and lyric poetry, Mint Edition books showcase the master works of our time in a modern new package. The text is freshly typeset, is clean and easy to read, and features a new note about the author in each volume. Many books also include exclusive new introductory material. Every book boasts a striking new cover, which makes it as appropriate for collecting as it is for gift giving. Mint Edition books are only printed when a reader orders them, so natural resources are not wasted. We're proud that our books are never manufactured in excess and exist only in the exact quantity they need to be read and enjoyed. To learn more and view our library, go to minteditionbooks.com

# bookfinity & MINT EDITIONS

Enjoy more of your favorite classics with Bookfinity,
a new search and discovery experience for readers.
With Bookfinity, you can discover more vintage
literature for your collection, find your Reader Type,
track books you've read or want to read,
and add reviews to your favorite books.
Visit www.bookfinity.com, and click on
Take the Quiz to get started.

Don't forget to follow us
@bookfinityofficial and @mint_editions